THE MOMENT OF TRUTH

Wiping his palms on his dirty pants, Ricky looked straight ahead. As soon as he cleared the big shed, he would be visible from the outhouse. There would be no time to taxi down and use the full runway. Takeoff toward the compound would give him the most distance and be into the wind. Even that might not be enough.

Well, this was it. Mouth dry as dirt, hands trembling, Ricky turned the ignition to START.

SPARROW HAWK RED
BEN MIKAELSEN

HYPERION PAPERBACKS FOR CHILDREN

New York

FIRST HYPERION PAPERBACK EDITION: September 1994

7 9 10 8

Library of Congress Cataloging-in-Publication Data
Mikaelsen, Ben
Sparrow Hawk Red/Ben Mikaelsen — 1st ed.
p. cm.
Summary: Thirteen-year-old Ricky, the Mexican-American son of a
former Drug Enforcement Agency man, tries to avenge his mother's
murder by crossing over into Mexico to steal a high-tech radar plane
from drug smugglers.
ISBN 1-56282-387-6 (trade) — ISBN 1-56282-388-4 (lib. bdg.)
ISBN 0-7868-1002-5 (pbk.)
[1. Adventure and adventurers — Fiction. 2. Mexico — Fiction.
3. Mexican Americans — Fiction. 4. Airplanes — Fiction.] 1. Title.
PZ7.M5926Sp 1993
[Fic]—dc20 92-53458 CIP AC

In memory of Daniel Mikaelsen,
my brother

1

Ricky Díaz drew back on the airplane's control stick. The Baby Great Lakes biplane responded, chomping hungrily at the air and roaring upward. Ricky feared pulling back too hard. This was his first loop alone, and today his dad, Benito Díaz, watched from the ground— a private landing strip on their southern Arizona ranch.

The loop didn't feel right. Was it rushed? Or waffled? One thing was certain. This time Dad was not in the front cockpit. His firm hand was not shadowing each movement through the dual controls. Gulping a nervous breath, Ricky relaxed pressure on the control stick. Instead of going over upside down, the biplane continued climbing straight up, bursting through a thin bank of clouds.

The big radial engine growled as the powerful biplane slowed. Drained of airspeed, the controls grew mushy, unresponsive. Wind blasting past the open cockpit disappeared. Still the propeller slashed at the air, and for a moment the straining twin-winged aircraft hung suspended.

Ricky panicked. He shoved the stick completely forward. No response, only an eerie calm. He jerked back. Then again he kicked the rudder pedals and jammed the stick ahead. Still nothing. Time froze. The powerful biplane shuddered and drifted backward. Raw fear tore at Ricky. This had never happened before. Suddenly the left wing dropped, and the biplane bucked over on its nose. Aimed nearly straight down, it started to spin. The engine thundered louder.

"Pull off the throttle, Ricardo." Benito spoke calmly through the headphones.

Ricky shoved and pulled at the stick. His dad's voice was calm, but he used the name Ricardo when something wasn't right.

"The throttle, Ricardo." Benito's voice hardened. "Do it!"

With the world twisting around faster and faster, Ricky tried to concentrate. He groped for the throttle handle, finally yanking it back. The engine quieted, but the spinning became more violent.

Benito's words crackled over the radio. "Now let go of the stick."

Ricky knew well what he should do, but it didn't feel right letting go of the stick. Not when the nose aimed straight down. Instead he panicked and pulled back.

"You're tightening the spin," Benito said, his voice calm but hard. "Do it—let go! Stop the spin first."

Ricky forced his hands off the stick.

2

"Good. Now step right rudder."

Ricky obeyed, stepping hard on the right pedal. The plane snapped out of the spin into a deadly dive. Air screamed and buffeted the biplane's wings like a mad beast.

"Okay, *now* pull back!"

Ricky grabbed the stick. Breathing hard, he pulled back. Speed kept building. The wind slapped hard at Ricky's shoulder-length black ponytail.

The Baby Great Lakes biplane howled downward. Using both arms, Ricky pried back even harder on the control stick. Although only thirteen years old, he made the wings strain. His cheeks sagged, and the pressure brought small, flickering black patches across his vision. It threatened to blind him.

The earth loomed ahead like a floating wall. Ricky blinked behind his flight goggles. He knew the earth wouldn't mind the crash of a shiny red biplane any more than it minded someone spitting into a gopher hole. And what loss would a scrawny, dark-skinned eighth grader be, too young for a flying license?

Ricky's eyelids were being forced closed by the pressure. He knew he had to finish pulling from the dive—otherwise his speed would keep building. The wings' tight support wires started whining. If one snapped, the wings could disintegrate into a thousand bits and shreds. The rest of the biplane would continue into the ground like a two-hundred-mile-per-hour bullet, with him in it!

Now the wind shrieked like an attacking cat. The pressure made Ricky's arms weigh a hundred pounds and his body a quarter ton. His chest felt as if an elephant stood on it. He clenched his teeth and clung to the stick.

Stubbornly, in slow motion, the big fields settled back underneath the wings. Ricky relaxed his grip. Gradually the elephant stepped off.

"Por qué lo dejaste?" said Benito. His dad wanted to know why Ricky had quit and backed out of the loop. He hadn't minded Ricky trying a loop, but before takeoff he had lectured, "If you try one, then do it! Quitting halfway through a maneuver is dangerous. If you quit, the sky won't respect you, and neither will I."

Ricky did not answer. The air didn't allow for quitters. Deep down Ricky knew he had quit. He hadn't pulled into the loop fast enough. Then he'd been afraid to go upside down. He'd waffled it and stalled.

Again his dad's voice crackled through the headset. "Why did you quit? The Baby wanted to loop." The Baby was what his dad called the Baby Great Lakes biplane.

Still Ricky did not answer. He looked up into the blue sky and thought of his mother. "I'll do it right next time, Mamá," he murmured. In his mind he could see her nodding and smiling.

"Do you hear me?" Benito said.

Ricky pushed the button for his headset. "Yes, Papá! I'll do it right next time," he stammered.

"In a trainer, there might not be a next time!" Benito snapped back, referring to the smaller planes—the little Cessnas and Pipers.

Puddle jumpers, Ricky thought. You had to wind up their rubber bands. Kid stuff! But he knew his dad was right. Without the Baby's power he might have ended up on his back in a flat spin. Or he might have pulled the wings off. But it was that power he loved. He hated the trainers. He'd never fly one of them again.

"What kind of wingman are you?" Benito added.

These words cut Ricky deeply. Once his dad had been a jet pilot in the air force, a fighter jockey. He often said he'd fly through the gates of hell if he trusted the man flying beside him—near his wing. A good wingman, he said, was never a quitter. I'll never be anybody's wingman, Ricky thought bitterly. Not Dad's. Not anybody's!

"Ven! Inmediatamente!" his father said, ordering him to return to the field.

Ricky had been raised calling his father Papá. That seemed natural. But it was silly how Dad spoke so much Spanish—he said it was part of their heritage. They were American citizens, born and raised in Arizona, Ricky thought. If Grandpa's dad had been raised in a chicken coop, would everybody have had to learn how to cluck?

Ricky banked into the wind and slipped the biplane down toward the runway. It gave him shivers just to feel the powerful aircraft move under his command. Wind buffeted him gently, whipping his ponytail against his bare neck. The landing was looking good. Wings level on final approach, he settled into a powered glide.

He and Dad lived out here alone. Mom had loved the country—the walks at sunset, flights in the Baby, roosters crowing at dawn. But she was gone. Dead. Killed in a car accident. After three years the memories of her had not softened or faded. Even now Ricky imagined her watching him.

Ricky never wanted to forget her. She was as real now

as when she left for the grocery store that day three years ago. She had asked Ricky if he wanted to go to town. Instead he went flying with Dad. Maybe somehow she wouldn't have died if he'd gone along.

Ricky glanced one last time at the gauges, then up. A movement at the far end of the runway caught his eye. A large car had parked between their sprawling brick house and the silver-painted hangar. Several men moved about. Ricky recognized the black sedan. Men from the DEA—the Drug Enforcement Agency—hadn't been around the house in a very long time.

After Dad left the air force, he had worked for the DEA, doing undercover work and flying patrol flights along the Mexican border. On weekends he flew the Baby Great Lakes in air shows for fun. But three years ago, after Mom died, he left the agency and retired to the ranch. At least that's what he'd called it. To Ricky it seemed more like quitting. Dad was too young to retire. He raised a few cows and farmed a little, but he didn't fly in air shows anymore.

Ricky remembered the maneuvers Dad used to "wring out" at shows. People in the crowd would gasp and hold their breath, then cheer wildly. Ricky always shouted, "That's my *papá*! That's my *papá*!" Back then, Ricky was sure Dad could have beaten even the Red Baron in a dogfight. Dad still did loops and rolls but not the wild and crazy stuff he did before the accident. Once he even flew upside down under a bridge.

After Mom's death, Dad started teaching Ricky to fly. It wasn't legal. But Dad said you didn't wait until you were grown to walk, talk, and breathe. So why should you wait to learn flying? Birds didn't. The real reason, Ricky suspected, was to help both of them forget about Mom. Whatever the reason, Ricky loved to fly the high-powered, aerobatic Baby Great Lakes biplane. So many times he wanted to tell his friends about his flying, but because he was only in eighth grade he couldn't. Dad said he had to wait until he turned fifteen and had his solo license.

The biplane hummed gently, drifting down out of the sky. Ricky pulled back the stick and flared the Baby smoothly onto the dirt strip. He hoped Dad had seen the smooth "greased" landing. As Ricky throttled back beside the hangar, his father kept limping toward the porch with the guests. Somehow Benito had lost a toe years ago after getting out of the air force—said it happened working with a baling machine.

Benito turned and made a knifing gesture with his hand, then entered the house with the three men. Obeying, Ricky cut the throttle. The big radial engine coughed smoke and shuddered to a halt.

After shoving blocks under the tires, Ricky headed for the house. What was up? Dad usually waited to help put away the plane. Had he forgotten about the stall and spin? No way!

Ricky entered the house and heard harsh voices in the study. Through the open door, he saw Benito standing quietly, his shoulders square and chin high. The three men, all in white shirts and ties, surrounded him. The loudest man was large and chubby, with a shiny bald head.

When they spotted Ricky approaching, the arguing

stopped. Another of the men, tall and thin, nodded with a grin. "Nice landing."

Ricky nodded back.

The loud, bald man interrupted, motioning Ricky away. "Go on, kid," he said. "We're talking to your dad."

Benito spun on the man. "Dexter, this is my house, and this is my son. I'll give orders around here." While the man stuttered, Benito turned. "Ricky, please go clean and fuel the Baby. I'll be done soon." Not waiting for a reply, he closed the door.

Ricky stood for a minute. Whoever that bald guy was and whatever he wanted, he was a jerk. Also, the look on his dad's face bothered Ricky—a mixture of anger and sadness. It was the same look that came over him when he talked about Mom. And that wasn't often.

Intense talking erupted, muted but growing louder and louder. The talking followed Ricky as he started toward the front door. Then he heard his father's muffled voice growl, "They killed my wife! Isn't that enough?"

An invisible hand clamped Ricky's throat and held him in the doorway. His breath came in short gasps. Mom murdered? Had he heard right? What was Dad talking about? Mom had died in a car accident; nobody killed her. Trembling, Ricky listened to the muffled voices. He heard the bald guy's voice. "Ah, come on. We don't know she was murdered."

"You don't know that, Dexter, because you don't want to," Benito said, his voice tense. "Makes it easier for you to go into your air-conditioned office each morning."

"Drop it, you two—that's a different issue!" barked a commanding voice.

"No, Frank!" said Benito. "It's not a different issue. I'm done with the DEA."

The same man spoke again. "Listen, Benito, you and

I go back a long way. You know I wouldn't be here if it wasn't important. Just hear me out."

There was silence. Then Benito spoke, his voice subdued. "Make it short."

Ricky strained to hear as he tiptoed back toward the study door. If Dad caught him listening, there would be more than a scolding.

The guy that Dad had called Frank continued. "In two weeks the president has a summit meeting with Guillermo Chávez, the president of Mexico. Chávez is requesting more foreign aid for their fight against drugs."

"What's that have to do with me?" Ricky heard Benito ask.

"After you left the agency," said Frank, "the military developed what we call a signature radar. As you know, most radars tell only approximate size, altitude, and location of an aircraft. But once a profile is recorded, the signature radar can pick an individual airplane out of a squadron of identical planes. It's dynamite. We learn the unique signature of each smuggler's plane, and the radar warns us whenever one crosses the border."

"Get to the point," Benito insisted.

The guy Frank kept talking. "Last year three of these radars were given to the Mexican government to help stop drug traffickers from bringing drugs into the United States. One month ago our number of smuggling intercepts on the border dried up. Every plane we approach turns tail and runs. At first I doubted it, but now I'm sure one of the signature radars has fallen into bad hands. Here, look."

Ricky could not tell what his father was being shown,

but the man continued. "These are screen recordings of the last ten intercepts. On each the target reversed course even before we changed our heading for intercept. Now look at this. . . . The outlying aircraft on each of these is different, except for down here. See this plane? It's on each screen recording, and it flies a holding pattern fifty miles inside their border. That's within the range of a signature radar. It's the only way they could know we're around.

"We've had agents check. The plane is an orange-and-white Cessna 172 Skyhawk, and it's based at a private strip on the Camacho cattle ranch just west of Mariposa. That ranch is a front for the León drug cartel. We're convinced one of our radars is actually on that plane and being used against us."

"I can't help you." Benito sounded bitter. "I'm not in the cop business anymore. Besides, I don't understand why you're even telling me this—I'm sure it's classified."

"Benito," said the third voice. "We need you to steal that aircraft."

"Steal it! Are you serious?"

"An active DEA agent could never enter Mexico and retrieve that plane without going through standard DEA procedures. That means notifying the Mexican *federales*—some of the very people we suspect. If they're not notified and we're caught, it blows apart the president's summit."

Dexter—the man who had been gruff to Ricky earlier—broke in, his gravelly voice sounding mean. "The State Department wants a pilot from outside the agency to infiltrate the drug compound and fly back the Sky-

11

hawk. The president needs absolute proof. And without risk."

"Yeah," said Benito. "No risk to him or you. But if I get caught, you never heard of me before, right?"

"We disclaim involvement," growled the man. "You know the rules."

"I've already lost my wife to this dirty business. I still have a son who needs me. Can't you see I'm through?"

"But you were the first to get close to the León cartel."

"Because I wasn't a lazy pencil pusher." Benito spoke accusingly.

"Don't look at me when you say that!" sounded the gruff voice.

"I'll look anywhere I darn well please. Listen, for God's sake, they killed my wife! Think what you're asking."

Ricky blinked back tears and swallowed to keep from choking. Killed? It wasn't a car accident! Someone killed Mom!

The commanding voice spoke more gently. "Benito, I'm asking you to just think about it. Maybe the León cartel did kill your wife. If so, this is your chance to strike back. You're Mex. You talk Spanish—you can go in and get this plane. We prove they have that radar, and it blows the lid clean off their operation."

"Gimme a break," said Benito Díaz. "You've been in your air-conditioned office too long. A Mexican drug compound isn't an open party where you stroll in if you have a good suntan. They're as tight as some prisons. Even if I wanted, I couldn't get in. Most important, I don't want to."

"But, Benito, think about—"

"Did you hear me? I said no! It's time for you to leave."

Before the study door could open, Ricky ran from the house and across the lawn toward the hangar. His mind raced as he pulled the hose from the gas barrel and started fueling the biplane. His hands shook. Over and over he spit at the ground. When he was younger he thought tears came from having too much water in the head. He'd learned to spit away the water to keep from crying. Sometimes it seemed to help.

The men strode from the house and soon sped away, tires spitting gravel back at Ricky's father. Dust hung in the air as Benito walked slowly across the lawn. His limp seemed worse.

Ricky could not keep his mind on fueling the plane. His mother killed? No! That's not what had happened. But he knew that it was true.

"*Mi 'jito,*" said his dad, approaching. He used the Spanish for "my son" kindly.

Thoughts jumbling, Ricky turned his head away.

"What's wrong?" asked Benito.

Ricky blinked at his tears and spit at the ground, continuing to hide his face.

"Look at me," ordered Benito.

Ricky turned and stammered, "Papá. . . . Nobody killed Mamá." Angry tears flooded out with his words. "Tell me no one killed her!"

3

Ricky stared at his father accusingly.

Benito looked down and brushed at something on his pants. "So, you were listening." When Ricky did not answer, Benito's voice softened. "Oh, *mi 'jito*," he said sadly. "I should have told you . . . but I was trying to protect you."

"Who . . . who killed Mamá? Why would they?" Ricky choked on his words.

Benito slid a gentle arm around his son's shoulder and led him out across the open desert. For several minutes he did not speak. "Three years ago," he said finally, "I was investigating the León cartel—a drug-smuggling operation south of the border near Mariposa. I got a phone call one night warning me to back off."

"Did you?"

Bunching his lips, Benito shook his head. "I didn't. And a week later your mother had the wreck. We found a loosened steering pin in the wreckage. The DEA thinks it was an accident, but I know in my heart it wasn't. I was the one they were after. It should have been me in that car."

"Why don't you go get the plane and pay them back for what they did?"

Benito stopped and looked down. "You listened to our whole talk, didn't you?"

Ricky avoided his father's stare.

"Losing your mother took the fight out of me," Benito said. "I'm done with the DEA."

Ricky didn't understand. "You always tell me not to be a quitter," he blurted. "Don't you miss Mamá?"

"I miss her dearly, *mi 'jito*," Benito said. "Every hour of every day. But stealing that plane won't bring her back."

"Stealing the plane can't be that hard. A 172 Skyhawk is just a big trainer. Papá, you're the one being a quitter."

"Stop this nonsense," Benito said sharply.

"You mean someone can kill Mamá and get away with it? Dad, a Skyhawk is easy to fly."

Benito shook his head, exasperated. "Ricky, you think the plane is sitting in a Kmart parking lot with the keys on the dashboard? This isn't a game. These men are killers! I couldn't steal it even if I wanted."

"Those DEA guys thought you could."

"They're looking for ways to keep the agency from being involved. They all know it's a suicide job. They like to think Mexican security is second-rate." Benito softened his voice, but still it was edged with bitterness. "They don't understand Mexican ways."

"If someone killed Mamá, you should go get the plane."

15

The sharpness returned to Benito's face. Then he shook his head. "Oh, *mi 'jito*. I—"

"Papá," Ricky interrupted. "You're always telling me not to quit—not to be a quitter. Then how come you, you . . ." Ricky's voice trailed off.

Benito struggled for words, then stopped. A slight smile crossed his face. "You want to talk about quitting, then let's go up there and talk about quitting." He pointed at the sky.

Ricky looked at his father, puzzled.

"Is the Baby full?" Benito asked.

The question caught Ricky off guard. He nodded. "Almost."

"Good. We're going to go up and have a talk about quitting."

Ricky's thoughts were not on flying. All he could think of was his mother and how somebody had killed her.

"Let's go!" Benito ordered.

Ricky didn't want to fly, but reluctantly he followed Benito toward the biplane.

"Do you want front or back?" Benito asked.

Most days they argued to sit in back—that was the control seat. The cockpits had dual controls, but the ignition and most of the instruments were in back. Without answering, Ricky crawled up front.

Benito walked around the Baby, giving her a quick preflight inspection. Usually they preflighted together: checking the flight surfaces, the fuel and oil, looking for nicks on the propeller, making sure the powerful little plane was ready for flight. Instead Ricky huddled in his seat. This was Dad's idea, let *him* get ready.

16

"How 'bout let's put on our shoulder harnesses?" Benito hollered, crawling into the rear cockpit.

The words caught Ricky's attention. If they went up for normal flight, they only put on the regular seat belts. But when Dad planned on looping or rolling the Baby, he insisted on wearing shoulder harnesses. He called it "chasing buzzards."

Ricky drew the heavy webbing down across his chest and snugged it tight. Normally a flight like this filled him with a fevered excitement. Today he felt empty. He felt like crying.

The starter coaxed the polished wood propeller over with a *thup, thup, thup*. Then a belch of white smoke erupted as the big radial engine growled to life. Ricky smelled the oily exhaust and heard the deafening roar. The dusty heat was suffocating. He slid his goggles on.

Benito tapped Ricky's shoulder and motioned toward his radio headset. The headsets allowed them to talk without letting go of the controls. Grudgingly, Ricky pulled on his headgear as they taxied to the runway. He didn't want to talk to anyone right now.

After warm-up, the Baby Great Lakes thundered down the runway, gaining speed. Blasts of air kicked up tumbleweed and dust in a small storm. Several short bounces cleared them from the ground, and the Baby started into a steep, hungry climb. Behind them the ocotillo and organ cactus looked like weeds. They flew in thick silence until the roads were threads stretched across the desert.

"Is your harness tight, *mi 'jito*?" Benito asked, his voice crackling over the headset.

Ricky tugged at his harness. Without looking back, he flashed the thumbs-up signal.

"Okay, grab your socks—it's show time!" Benito snapped the Baby into a long series of rolls. Around and around they flipped. The harness grabbed at Ricky's shoulders each time they twisted upside down. Ricky rested his hand on the control stick but only so he could feel his dad's strong hand moving deftly, one with the plane—not shoving or forcing but guiding and encouraging the powerful machine. Dad made it seem so easy.

Air whipped past the open cockpit. The wings leveled, and Ricky barely caught his breath before the nose pitched forward, starting a long, whining outside loop. Dad hadn't done one of these in years.

Unlike inside loops, which drained blood from the head and sometimes caused blackouts, an outside loop surged blood into the head, causing redouts. Ricky hung upside down. Gravity tugged hard to pull him out of the biplane. The harness webbing bit into his shoulders. Crimson patches flooded his vision. People who didn't fly would never understand how great his body felt at times like this. It was more fun than anything he had ever known. His whole body grinned under the pressure. This was living!

Finishing the outside loop, Benito nosed the Baby into a long, gliding dive. They settled easily down through the sky. "You see that saguaro cactus ahead to the left?" Benito said.

Ricky couldn't avoid grinning. He reached into a zippered pouch beside the seat and pulled out a small paper bag filled with flour. "Milk shake says I get closer," he yelled.

"You're first," Benito said, his voice raspy over the headset.

"No! Go ahead," Ricky answered.

"Okay." Benito guided the biplane straight at the cactus in a shallow dive. Ricky peered back. His father held his paper bag outside the open cockpit. The trick was in guessing when to release the little bag. It never fell straight down. At a hundred and forty miles per hour, you had to drop the bag early, lobbing it toward the target. This game used to be a bit wilder. For years Dad dive-bombed neighbors' cars. After Ricky started flying, they changed to road crossings and desert cactus. Benito didn't want to teach bad habits.

Wind grabbed at Benito's arm. Suddenly he let go. The little packet was snatched away. He pulled out of the dive and banked sharply to the right. Ricky squinted down. Below on the desert floor a small puff of white blossomed about a hundred feet short of the cactus.

"Hah! Beat that," Benito said.

Ricky took the controls. It was easiest for him to hold the bag of flour in his teeth as he climbed. Cutting the throttle, Ricky eased the Baby into a long, shallow dive, aimed directly at the same saguaro cactus. Easy, he told himself. Not yet . . . wait . . . wait. Air buffeted his face. He kept the nose glued to the target on the desert floor. Easy. Not yet. Looming larger, the big saguaro cactus stood, trunks branching out, like a giant showing off its muscles. Just a second longer, Ricky thought.

Okay . . . now!

He grabbed the bag from his teeth and threw it into the rushing air, then pulled from the dive and banked sharply. Long seconds passed before another small patch of white mushroomed on the desert floor—closer to the cactus. Ricky let out a whoop and felt a good-natured slap on his shoulder.

As they climbed back up, Ricky thought of another game Benito had taught him. Years before, during training in a small, closed-cockpit Cessna 150, Benito would dive the trainer as fast as a person would fall. For a few seconds they became weightless. Then he released a marshmallow. As he controlled the dive, the marshmallow floated magically about the cockpit. It took great skill, but before switching over to the Baby Great Lakes, Ricky had floated a marshmallow into Dad's mouth.

Because he wasn't allowed to tell friends he could fly, Ricky couldn't explain the excitement of feeding Dad a marshmallow. Things like that had to stay his secret.

"Now, about quitting!" Benito shouted, not offering to take back control of the Baby.

The words surprised Ricky. "What about it?" he answered bluntly.

"Let's see a real loop."

Ricky felt angry. "I'll show you the best loop in Arizona," he snapped as he pulled into a climb. He'd learned to talk cool by listening to Dad. Pilots never spoke as if they were scared.

The climb to altitude gave Ricky time to rehearse everything in his mind. Once into the loop, there wasn't time to think. It had to be automatic. And this loop he wouldn't waffle. At three thousand feet, Ricky leveled off.

Benito spoke. "Be deliberate, *mi 'jito*."

"Call me Son," Ricky said. "Not *mi 'jito*!"

There was a moment of silence; then Benito added, "Don't rush it, don't waffle it. Just do it! Announce it! Tell every lizard and buzzard in Arizona what you're planning."

Ricky eased the control stick forward, dipping the nose to gain speed. Into the rushing air he screamed, "I'm no quitter! You hear me, lizards? Here's a fat loop—you better duck." With those words he pulled back on the stick.

This time Ricky kept pulling hard as the nose pitched skyward. Rocketing straight up, he fought the urge to back out. He held the pressure, feeling his body become nearly weightless as they went upside down. Then the plane nosed earthward.

Deliberately he reached out, cutting the throttle. Extra speed would only make the last half harder. From here on it was a tug-of-war against gravity. Quickly speed built, and Ricky grunted against the invisible hand squeezing air from his chest. He blinked at the black patches that flickered and tried to blind him. By entering the loop deliberately, Ricky did not have to struggle as hard coming out of the dive. Soon he leveled the Baby.

Benito slapped his shoulder and motioned a thumbs-up signal. "You'd make a good wingman!" he shouted.

"Not yours," Ricky snapped back. "I'm no quitter!" He half expected a sharp, reprimanding swat to his head.

21

Instead there was hurt silence. Benito did not offer to take back the controls. Ricky banked the plane back toward the ranch. He shouldn't have said what he did.

Off the left wing a milky white cloud loomed like a small mountain. Ricky banked the Baby along the edge of the white billowy wall, extending his arm to touch it. The solid-looking cloud turned to fog as he neared. It always did. But still Ricky dreamed that someday his hand would fill with a soft white cotton that he could put in his pocket and save.

On the horizon, the landing strip grew larger. Ricky drew in long deep breaths of fresh air as they descended. He throttled back until the thunder of the big radial engine turned into a muted hum. The Baby drifted down for a perfect landing. Ricky could not see the proud smile on his dad's face.

After landing, neither of them spoke until the Baby was "tucked in." Then, walking slowly to the house, Benito reached out and hugged Ricky's shoulders. "Nice loop. That's one to be proud of."

Ricky could not help feeling proud. "I'll bet Chuck Yeager or John Glenn would have liked it," he said quietly.

"You bet. And so would the Aztecs and the Mayans. And the Mixtecs and the Olmecs—"

"I know, I know," Ricky mimicked. "And the Toltecs and the Zapotecs. Did I forget any?" He had heard this pitch before. These were his ancestors.

"Yes, you did. There was Montezuma and Zapata . . . and hundreds more. Don't forget them. They would be proud of you. So be proud of them." Benito drew Ricky into his strong arms as if hugging the invisible people. "Feel them, Ricardo, feel them. They were brave people. They made you what you are. Remember them."

"I'll bet Mamá saw the loop," Ricky said, pushing away from his dad.

Benito did not answer.

The shock and the hurt crashed back in around Ricky. Someone had killed his mother. It felt as if she had died all over again. Why didn't Dad do something?

Ricky wanted to be alone. He went straight to his room, closed the door, and flopped down on his big water bed. He looked around at the walls covered with posters: an F-14 Tomcat like the one Dad had flown, a Ford Tri-Motor, the space shuttle *Discovery*, a Grumman Goose, and his favorite—a picture of the gleaming red Baby with him in the cockpit. Today the posters failed to cheer him.

Getting up, he walked to the window and looked out across the desert toward the Mexican border. Somewhere west of Mariposa was the Camacho cattle ranch and an orange-and-white Cessna 172 Skyhawk. The plane was just a four-person model of the Cessna 150 he had trained in. It would be easy to fly. An idea pried at his thoughts. How could a thirteen year old get close? For a long time Ricky stared out the window, his thoughts churning. Was there any way he could steal the Skyhawk?

4

Ricky could not think of a way to steal the Skyhawk. He puzzled till his head hurt, then crossed to the dresser and did what he had done many times over the last three years. He pulled a photo album from the bottom drawer and returned to sit on the edge of his bed. Trembling, he turned the pages.

One picture showed Mom, Dad, and him in swimming suits by the ocean. Dad had dark brown skin and hair and looked funny in a swimming suit—like a bulldozer. Mom had soft, lighter skin and blond hair. Ricky didn't like looking at the picture of himself. His ribby chest, bony shoulders, and big cheekbones made him look like a skeleton.

Several pages later Ricky stopped and stared at another picture. This one was taken at the county fair. He had just won twenty-five dollars in a pig-wrestling contest. He would never have won by wrestling like most of the other kids; grabbing the biggest greased oinker and trying to muscle it across the line. He had been too small. He won by using his head. He ran to the smallest pig, a fifty-pounder, and grabbed a hoof. He'd figured out that the hooves weren't greased. Gripping hard, he was able to drag the jerking and squealing pig across the line.

In the picture, Mom stood beside him wearing her favorite yellow dress, making him look even more dirty. His grubby body was almost unrecognizable, but Mom was hugging him, her thin arm wrapped tightly around his shoulders. She hadn't cared about the mud or whether she wore a good dress.

"They shouldn't have killed you, Mamá," Ricky cried softly, gripping the photo album with white knuckles. His mom stared back up from the page, smiling. How could anyone have killed someone so kind and gentle? So pretty?

Dad shouldn't have refused to go after the plane, Ricky thought. Benito could cross the border and not stand out like a gringo. The longer Ricky studied the picture, the deeper an idea snagged in his mind. He looked much like the street children he'd seen in Mexico. Why couldn't he go down and pretend to be a *ratero*, or street rat, as he called them?

Sure, it sounded crazy. But that was exactly why it might work. A young *ratero* could get close to the Camacho cattle ranch. Who would be expecting a homeless boy to steal an airplane? After chewing on the thought awhile, Ricky swallowed it.

"Mamá," he said aloud. "I'll go and act like I'm a

ratero. I won't let them get away with what they did to you." He sniffled back tears and imagined her speaking.

"Oh, bunk!" she said. That was how Mom spoke. "Don't you call those kids *rateros*. They're not street rats! They're just like you, only they've had bad luck. Now, you get your schoolwork done and quit worrying about me."

For the first time rebellion crept into Ricky's mind. Mom never wanted anyone to fuss or bother over her. Well, that was just tough. He had a plan, and nobody could stop him. It all seemed simple. Dress up as a *ratero*—and they *were* street rats, he thought to himself. Then sneak up to the Skyhawk and fly it home. There were things he would have to figure out, like how to get there. Would there be guards? What if someone caught him? The more he puzzled over the plan, the less simple it all seemed.

Ricky stayed alone in his room, thinking. Once during the evening, Benito knocked on the door. "Ricky," he said gently. When there was no answer he called again. "Ricky."

"Go away!" Ricky yelled. "Go away and leave me alone."

After a long pause, footsteps faded down the hallway.

Ricky didn't blame Dad for Mom's death. But why didn't Dad do something? Why didn't he go after the airplane? No matter what got said, Dad was being a quitter. A low-down quitter!

And this was the worst kind of quitting, Ricky thought. Dad had a choice. It wasn't like getting beaten up at school. Ricky remembered one particularly bad whupping he'd gotten from some bullies. Two big ninth graders had cornered him. While several kids stood and watched, the two bullies pounded him until his face was puffy and his lips swollen. When Ricky could no longer fight back, the big boys stood over him. "You quitter!" they yelled again and again. "Get up and fight!"

One grabbed him by his long hair and dragged him in circles on his knees. A hard yank sent him sprawling. The bully held up a strand of Ricky's ink black hair and laughed.

Ricky had wanted so badly to prove he wasn't a quitter. When he tried to get up, they knocked him down again, still laughing. If only they knew he was a pilot, they wouldn't laugh, Ricky thought. He didn't dare tell them, though. Nor did he dare tattle to Dad. That would only make it worse. Then he would be a squealer. Nothing he did that day could prove he wasn't a quitter.

But today was different. Today he could do something.

Before going to bed, Ricky pulled his small gym bag from the closet. In it he stuffed a tattered old pair of blue jeans and a dirty, ripped T-shirt. Most Mexicans lived and dressed very well, but not the *rateros*. They slept on the sidewalks and went barefoot, wearing rags for clothes. Ricky's feet weren't tough enough to go barefoot. Even his oldest pair of tennis shoes weren't real old, but he threw them in.

Two more things might help.

First, his photo ID, just in case he couldn't steal the plane. Mexican customs seldom checked anyone coming into their country. Coming back across, however, U.S. Immigration would ask to see identification.

Second, his jackknife. A knife would help him cut and strip wires to get the airplane started. This was something he'd learned helping Dad install an ignition switch on the Baby Great Lakes. He hoped a Skyhawk would be the same. He put the knife and ID card into his bag.

Not able to think of anything else, he crawled into bed. He lay awake thinking. What difference did it make if Mom died accidentally or was killed? Either way, she was dead—nothing would bring her back. Ricky's anger refused that notion. Stealing the plane was something he needed to do. He'd do it for Mom. And because he wasn't a quitter!

Thoughts of a crashing car, of airplanes, and of grubby *rateros* tumbled in his head. Even after the moon disappeared above the window, he still could not sleep. The lighted clock radio on the dresser displayed each minute forever. Ricky watched the hours pass. When dawn finally glowed into the room, he dozed off.

He dreamed he was at Kitty Hawk, sitting in the Wright brothers' kitelike biplane, getting ready to prove to the world that he could fly. With men running along holding the wingtips, he started his roll down the rail. Faster and faster and faster. He tried to be gentle on the controls as he rose into the sky. He floated up and kept floating, like a bird. He was free!

Then he dreamed he was Chuck Yeager, sitting in the Bell X-1, getting ready to try and break the sound barrier. Nobody had ever gone the speed of sound. Some said it would kill you—your body would blow up and pop like a balloon. Others said the pressure would crush you. Nobody knew for sure. Everybody waited and watched.

A large transport plane released the Bell X-1 rocket plane from the bay, and Ricky reached forward and ignited the rockets. It felt like a mule kicked him in the back. Faster and faster he flew. Five hundred, five-fifty, six hundred, six-fifty, some ominous shaking, the rocket roared loudly, severe vibration, six-eighty, the instruments blurred, still faster, six-ninety. A sharp thump. And then only smooth and eerie silence.

"Up and at 'em, lazybones. Time for school!" Benito called. "I'm headed to town; I'll give you a ride."

Ricky jarred awake and rolled from the bed. "Okay," he groaned, yawning hard. His skull felt numb, and he rubbed his sore eyes. It was hard to organize his jumbled thoughts. This morning everything had to seem normal. Stretching, he squirmed into his school clothes and combed his long hair back off his shoulders.

Dishes clinked in the kitchen. Ricky tiptoed to the hall closet. He and Dad kept a shoe box with Mexican pesos. Whenever they visited Mexico they used money from this stash instead of going through an exchange at the border. Ricky pulled down the box. There appeared to be quite a bit of money. He reminded himself that three thousand pesos equaled roughly one dollar. The handful of bills he had scooped up probably didn't amount to twenty dollars. Carrying around Mexican money was fun. Big wads of money made Ricky feel rich, at least until he had to buy something. It seemed like a gyp when a bottle of pop cost a thousand pesos.

Ricky stuffed the bills into his pocket and walked into the kitchen to join his dad. For a moment neither spoke.

Benito broke the ice. "How are you feeling this morning?"

"Pretty good," Ricky answered casually. Throughout breakfast, though, he avoided further talk. He was too tired to think clearly, and he didn't want to say anything that might make Dad suspicious.

After eating, Benito picked up Ricky's gym bag. "We better get hopping; school starts in about twenty minutes. Do you have everything you need here?"

Ricky held his breath and nodded. Together they walked out the door and across the yard. The gym bag swung loosely in Benito's hand. Ricky eyed it and fought the urge to grab it. If it felt too heavy or if the jackknife rattled, Dad might look inside. When Benito crawled into the old Ford pickup, he tossed the bag onto the seat between them. Ricky pulled the bag close and guarded it with his arm, letting out a relieved breath.

As the pickup bounced along the three-mile rutted road to town, Benito glanced over. "Do you want to go flying after school?"

"No." Ricky kept gazing out at the desert. The mesquite, cactus, and desert willow stretched for miles. He smiled to himself. He'd go flying sure enough but without Dad. And without the Baby Great Lakes. The day's pale blue sky and low winds made it perfect for flying. Benito hit the brakes, and Ricky looked forward. A roadrunner had dashed across the road and down into the ditch. Head ducked, it scurried off among the brittlebush. After all the years watching cartoons, Ricky half expected roadrunners to go *"beep, beep!"* They actually did make a kind of honking sound. More like *"br-rack, br-rack!"*

Nearing town, Benito interrupted the thick silence. "It hurts, doesn't it?"

Ricky didn't answer.

"Your mother's dying is a deep wound. Let it heal," Benito said. "Getting angry won't make the pain go away."

Ricky didn't like the comparison. This was a lot worse than a wound. But using the same reasoning, he shot back, "Yeah, and if you don't take care of it, it gets infected and never heals."

Benito bit at his bottom lip in thought. "You're still thinking about the DEA agents and that airplane, aren't you?" he said.

Ricky turned his head away, afraid anything he said might give away his plan.

"Ricky, I'm not being a quitter. If I went after that airplane, it wouldn't solve or heal anything. Can't you see that? You have to let your mother go." They drove on in silence. When the pickup pulled to a stop in front of the school, Ricky slid out. "Do you want me to pick you up?" Benito asked. "Or do you want to take the school bus home?"

"I'll get home on my own." Ricky slammed the door closed. Dad would have tadpoles if he knew what that meant.

"Okay, have a good day. I'll see you this afternoon. . . . Oh, don't forget this, *mi 'jito.*" Benito handed the gym bag out the window.

31

Ricky swallowed to keep from choking. He'd nearly forgotten the bag. What a slick move! How would he ever sneak a high-tech radar and airplane out of a drug compound if he couldn't remember a bag of old clothes? He had to wake up. Start thinking. Ricky grabbed the bag.

Benito smiled warmly.

Ricky met his smile with an accusing stare. "Dad, I don't like being called *mi 'jito*. It makes me sound like a little kid."

A pained look flickered in Benito's eyes.

Ignoring it, Ricky turned and walked toward the school. When the pickup rounded the corner out of sight, Ricky broke into a run toward the bus stop two blocks away. He arrived, panting heavily. A group of people stood waiting, looking bored. Still breathing hard, Ricky fidgeted with the handle of his gym bag—if people only knew what he had planned.

Soon a bus pulled to the curb, brakes screeching. Passengers pushed and shoved as they climbed aboard. Each had to drop change into the slot before crowding to the back. As Ricky worked his way down the aisle, he tried to think clearly. Skipping school seemed wrong. And so did stealing an airplane.

It was tempting to turn back—there was still time, no one would know. Memory of the pig-wrestling picture popped into his head. Mom would know if he quit. She would always know. He had to give it an honest try. This was the only way he could think of to make things right.

The bus rattled across town. At the south end of the

route, Ricky filed off behind other passengers. The border crossing waited only a few hundred feet away. A line of people jostled to pass through the checkpoint. Among the mostly Mexican crowd, a few Americans stood out, their clothes bright as Christmas tree ornaments. Ricky felt like one of the tourists with his long hair and good clothes. One thing made him different. He looked at his brown hands. His dark skin was the key to his plan.

The customs agent barely glanced up as Ricky moved through the turnstile. A sign on the wall read Welcome to Mexico.

5

The border town of Domingo hummed with activity. People crowded along the sidewalks, whistling, shouting, and laughing. Cars raced down the narrow streets, honking for no apparent reason. Ricky liked the commotion of Mexican border towns. Peppered meat sizzled at corner taco stands. Accordions, trumpets, and guitars filled the air with *ranchera* music. Ricky turned to watch a car drive by, the blaring loudspeaker on its roof advertising specials of the day for a local grocery store. Here every day seemed like a carnival.

Ahead was the marketplace. Ricky loved to rummage through the colorful stands and barter for things. In Mexico, if you paid the price asked, they acted disappointed. The merchants loved to dicker and haggle over every peso as if it were their last drop of blood. Ricky enjoyed this. Why couldn't the same thing happen back home? Why not have fun doing ordinary things?

Today there was no time to stop. Ricky passed by the market, hiking instead toward the highway south of town. On the way he passed by a car wash—not a real car wash, just an old man sitting beside four garden hoses, hoping to collect some money. A family with nine children pulled up in an old car. Each child jumped out, grasping a small patch of rag.

Ricky stopped and watched. As the father sprayed the hose at the car, his wife and herd of children scrubbed furiously. The man made no effort to avoid spraying his family, and soon all were drenched. Ricky half envied them—the heat made the cold water look inviting. When they finished, the dripping family piled back into their car and left.

Ricky kept walking. After reaching the highway, he waited. And waited. An hour passed before a bus rumbled by headed south to Mariposa. Ricky waved it down the way the Mexicans did. Calling the rattling pile of tin a bus was like calling an outhouse a castle. In fact, the Spanish name, *camión pollero*, meaning "chicken truck," was more accurate. The *camión pollero* swayed to a dusty stop on the shoulder. Its front door stood open. People and their belongings hung out the windows. At the front a heavy lady reclined sideways, filling a whole seat. A naked baby sat on her lap, crying with intense, hiccuping screams.

"*Doce mil pesos,*" said the driver, asking for twelve thousand pesos. He watched curiously as Ricky fumbled with the roll of bills. After peeling off the exact amount, Ricky squeezed past the big lady and worked his way down the aisle. Several passengers held wire cages on their laps. Inside were frightened chickens and rabbits. All seats were filled, so Ricky remained standing. Also standing were two women who balanced small bundles on their heads. One of the ladies had no teeth. She turned to look at Ricky with a gummy, curious smile.

The bus lurched forward, gears grinding. Dry, suffocating dust churned up from the gravel shoulder. No one seemed to mind. Ricky coughed as the bus rattled and wound down the road and across the Sonora Desert. Lowering his head, he glanced out the window.

The desert here was different from back home. Clumps of bear grass poked up from the sea of golden gramma grass. Only a few organ and saguaro cactus stood alone on the flats. A light wind rolled tumbleweed down the ditch, bouncing it lazily. Most people imagined a desert differently from this. Ricky's cousins from Chicago had visited last summer, expecting sand dunes and camels. Instead they found miles of thin grass and cactus. In every direction, groups of mountains rimmed the horizon like islands in the sky. Scrub oak and dusty green mesquite filled the open spaces.

In the high country, Ricky had seen mountain lions, bears, even bighorn sheep. Down here he mostly saw smaller critters like jackrabbits, skunks, ground squirrels, and pack rats. Right now he could see a column of buzzards to the south circling lower and lower—probably lured down by a sick or dying animal.

Ricky shifted his balance back and forth to rest his feet. When seats became vacant, he motioned for the standing ladies to sit down. Mom had been real big on being polite. Passengers whistled and hooted at his chivalry, watching him with curiosity. Ricky disliked this about his life: north of the border his toast-colored skin often got him teased. Here his upbringing and habits made him a stranger. He felt caught between the two worlds.

Clinging to his gym bag, he wrinkled his nose. Fresh fruits and peppers from the market did little to cover up the smell of animals, sweaty bodies, and wet diapers. Mixed with dust, the air became suffocating.

The fifty-mile trip to Mariposa lasted all morning. Ricky's legs grew tired of standing. The bus stopped often, allowing passengers to squirm off or squeeze on. A long bell-cord extended back through rings above the windows on both sides of the bus. When people wanted to stop they pulled the cord. Ricky wondered how the bus driver could hear the bell above the deafening clamor.

On the horizon, the whitewashed and red-tiled adobe buildings of Mariposa appeared, shimmering in the heat waves and growing larger. Ricky had been through Mariposa before and recognized the flood tunnel crossing under the highway a mile out from town. The big culvert would make a good place to change clothes. He quickly pulled the cord. The bus brakes screeched as he gripped his way up the aisle.

"Where does the brown gringo live? With the rabbits and lizards?" a young man joked in Spanish.

"Maybe he's lost," murmured an older lady.

It irked Ricky that they talked openly about him. He wished he didn't know Spanish. But Benito insisted on speaking it at home for weeks at a time to make sure he

37

didn't get rusty. So he wouldn't forget his heritage! After those long periods, Ricky actually found himself thinking in Spanish. He felt betrayed by his own mind.

People watched curiously as he stepped from the bus. Who could blame them? After all, why was a well-dressed American boy getting off the bus a mile from town on the open desert? As the bus pulled away, passengers eyed him through the billowing exhaust. Ricky looked down and pretended to walk nonchalantly along the shoulder.

When he reached the large culvert, he dropped into the ditch. Heavy silt covered the floor of the long tunnel. The ground was wrinkled with bone-dry cracks, although a *chubasco* could change that real quick. *Chubascos* were flash storms. Their black, billowing clouds rolled in unexpectedly, shaking the ground with thunder and lightning. In minutes, sheets of drenching rain dumped from the sky, flooding desert arroyos. Often people died when the sudden gully-washing walls of water cascaded down the stony river bottoms.

A stray cat shot out of the culvert. It held a scorpion in its mouth. Ricky jumped sideways. The scorpion's tail flicked back and forth, jabbing into the cat's cheek. She paid little notice as she scampered into the dried grass. A scorpion sting never seemed to harm a cat the way it did a person.

Ricky remembered being stung once. For two days his foot swelled, and he burned with fever. Mom sat holding his hand and singing to him softly. Today there would be no one to care for him or sing to him.

He squinted into the culvert, looking for other crit-ters—shade was a popular place on a desert. It looked empty. Ricky made sure no cars were coming, then ducked into the darkened, chest-high tunnel. He had to stoop to keep from hitting his head. Awkwardly he peeled off his good clothes. Crouching naked, he pulled the ragged clothes from the gym bag and wrestled them on. Last, he slipped the old tennis shoes over his bare feet. *Rateros* seldom wore shoes, and surely not socks. For all the effort, Ricky wondered if he looked much like a *ratero*. He didn't feel like one.

Deliberately he spread his belongings on the ground. Only forty-five thousand pesos were left—about fifteen dollars. He wadded the bills and stuffed them into his pocket along with the jackknife and ID card. His good clothes fitted into the small gym bag. If the airplane wasn't at the Camacho ranch, it would be good to have something to wear back across the border.

Ricky grabbed a handful of dirt and dusted his jeans and shoes. Then, eyes and mouth shut tightly, he rubbed several handfuls on his face and into his hair. This helped but not enough. His neatly trimmed hair needed more than messing up.

On the highway, oil stains showed where cars or *ca-miones polleros* had broken down—and they often did, especially the chicken trucks. Ricky smeared his fingers across a patch and rubbed the greasy filth into his hair, smudging some on his cheeks and clothes.

What if Mom saw him like this? He tried talking to her. "How do I look, Mamá?" he asked, stepping out of the culvert. At times like this his mother seemed so real. He imagined her looking down at him, studying him head to foot.

"You surely do look a mess," she said, smiling.

"Do you think I can steal the airplane dressed like this, Mamá?" he asked. Closing his eyes helped get her to answer.

"Is that what you're planning?" she said.

"Yup. They'll think I'm a *ratero*. They won't know I'm a pilot."

"Why are you saving your good clothes and your ID card?"

"In case I can't steal the plane," Ricky blurted, looking up. "Then I can still get home." He stooped down and started digging with his hands in the dirt to bury the gym bag.

"Looks to me like you're keeping a foot on first base while you try to steal second," she said.

"This isn't baseball," Ricky said, irritated. He imagined his mother shaking her head patiently.

"You either plan to succeed or you plan to fail," she said quietly. "If you're planning to fail, then go back. Stay on first base." Her voice became a whisper. "That would be safer."

Ricky ignored her and kept digging until he had a hole big enough for the gym bag. Then he stopped. Would this really make him quit if the going got rough? He wiped his hands on his pants and looked up. Could Mom be right? Maybe this was like waffling a loop—it would actually make him fail.

Trembling as if a small earthquake shook under him,

he stood and kicked dirt back into the hole. The picture flashed into his mind of Mom hugging him—the mud from pig wrestling hadn't mattered to her. It could have been manure, and she'd have still hugged him.

Quietly he spoke. "I don't plan on failing, Mamá." Picking up the bag, he started throwing his good clothes out along the highway. In no time they would be picked up. With each piece the distance home grew greater and greater. One last fling sent the gym bag spinning out into the golden gramma grass.

It felt good, but still there were things that would make him fail. He pulled out his ID card and ripped it up. The jackknife and money he would keep; he might need them for stealing the airplane. Still he knew that one thing was anchoring his foot to first base.

He pulled out his jackknife and opened it. For a moment the situation rubbed him funny. What in the world was he doing on a school day, here in the desert fifty miles south of the border, with ragged clothes on and a knife opened in his hand? He laughed, but he felt like crying.

He spit to keep back his tears and grabbed a handful of hair. No *ratero* would have hair like this. Afraid his courage might fade, Ricky chopped and cut frantically. Handful after handful fell to the ground. Finally all the long hair had been hacked short. No longer could he walk freely back through the border check station—his foot was off first base. Nobody would recognize him. Even if that was what he had wanted, the thought made him miserable and lonely. He'd thrown away his pride. Another thought bothered him. Who was he now? An

American? A *ratero*? Deep down, was he really a quitter?

Ricky returned the jackknife to his pocket and started walking toward Mariposa. Against the ditch bank, his shadow looked strange. He kicked dirt at it. Still it stayed beside him. Finally Ricky spit at the shadow and turned his head away from it.

After dropping Ricky off at school, Benito drove slowly. Thoughts of his son hung over him like a dark cloud. Why couldn't it be like old times? For years he had called Ricky his wingman, his most trusted buddy. And his son had announced proudly to any visitors, "I'm Papá's wingman!" But since his mother's death, Ricky had drawn inward, guarding his feelings. He rebuffed any mention of wingman.

Ricky had never been able to forget about his mother. Not that Benito had himself. But he had kept secret that he believed she was murdered—a death could destroy more than one person if you let it. Often he overheard Ricky still talking to his mother as if she existed. Her death had created a stubborn wall between him and his son. If only Ricky had not overheard the conversation with the DEA agents at the ranch house. No death was easy to deal with, but the murder of a mother . . .

Benito headed across town to pick up a new wheel bearing for the biplane. The Baby Great Lakes needed work if they were going flying this afternoon. Flying seemed to be the only thing that helped either of them forget the past. The only thing that helped them get along.

Today Ricky had insisted he didn't want to go flying. Benito was sure, though, that his son would change his mind after seeing the biplane standing ready. He always did. Flying the Baby was Ricky's greatest passion. His escape.

A hard white sun climbed high in the sky. Benito picked up mail at the mailbox, then pulled in to the yard and headed for the house. Inside, the red light flashed on his telephone answering machine. He rewound the tape. Several messages played while he sorted through the mail.

Beep————"Yeah, Benito. This is Ed. Do you mind if I borrow your post shovel tomorrow? I'll be over in the morning. Thanks."

Beep————"Mr. Díaz. This is Fix-Rite Auto. I have your generator rebuilt. It's ready to pick up whenever you're in town. Any questions, call me. Have a nice day."

Benito slapped the counter. He could have picked the generator up this morning if he'd known.

Beep————"Hello. This is the attendance office at Alamo Junior High School. Your son, Ricky, was reported absent today. It would help our office if you would notify us when your child is going to be absent. We do hope he's not ill. Please send a note with him when he returns."

Benito stared with surprise at the answering machine. Absent from classes? What in blazes? It couldn't be—she must be wrong. Quickly he dialed the school.

No, they insisted, Ricky Díaz had not shown up for classes. Benito hung up, his thoughts racing. If Ricky played hooky regularly, this might be expected. But never once had he pulled a stunt like skipping school. There was something defiant and foreboding about it. Something terribly wrong.

Instinctively he ran to Ricky's room. Nothing appeared out of place. If his son had run away, surely there would be a note. Finding out his mother was murdered had to have been a terrible shock for Ricky. He was probably walking alone somewhere, working things out.

Benito tried to recall what Ricky had said or done that might lend a clue. His son had few friends—places he could go. He was not one to go somewhere and just hang out. Benito shook his head—nothing made sense. Hopefully Ricky hadn't done anything foolish. The two of them were much alike, and that worried Benito the most. His own bum foot was a prime example. Benito still walked with a slight limp on account of losing his temper.

Years before, a beady-eyed pack rat had kept finding its way into the house, avoiding any poison or trap. The rat started crawling up on the bed at night. It would cross the wooden frame while making its rounds. Angry, Benito left a dim night-light glowing. When he heard the telltale scratching on the frame, he reached over and picked up his .38 revolver off the nightstand. Dimly the big rodent became visible as it crossed the foot rail.

Benito rested the revolver on his lap, aimed carefully, then fired. Besides blowing the rat into rat heaven, he also succeeded in shooting off his own little toe. Ricky had only been told it was a ranching accident.

Benito glanced helplessly around his son's room. Where was the boy? He reached for the phone to call the police, then stopped. He always lectured Ricky to think before reacting foolishly. Now he needed to do the same.

No kid would want to go to school after discovering that his mother had been murdered. Ricky was a thinker and didn't like showing his feelings. It made sense that he might skip school and go somewhere to be alone. Benito had to give his son that breathing space. Time would heal the wound. Surely Ricky would come home this afternoon on the school bus. Deliberately, Benito set to work on chores around the ranch.

As he worked, the notion of being a quitter crowded his thoughts. He hadn't quit the DEA, he had retired. And why not? Even before the accident, he had considered retirement—he had enough years in to draw a pension. Ricky's accusation that he was a quitter was absurd. Going after the León drug cartel was suicide—they were a ruthless organization! They needed to be stopped, but now it was somebody else's job. Benito didn't want Ricky to lose his father, too.

Again and again Benito reasoned through his actions. But he could not clear from his head the ringing of Ricky's words: "You're a quitter!" It made Benito more and more angry. Didn't Ricky see, nothing would bring back the dead!

Midafternoon found Benito in the hangar, checking his watch and glancing nervously out the drive. His anger still brewed as he paced back and forth beside the shiny biplane. Finally the school bus shimmered into view, stirring up dust in the heat waves. It appeared to slow, and Benito held his breath. Then the gears shifted, and the yellow bus lumbered on past.

Panic stunned Benito. Was it possible that the Drug Enforcement Agency had something to do with this? No, he decided. He had differences with them, but they were not a bad outfit. In fact, Frank Page and the rest were good men, except for the whiner, Dexter Crumm—the one who had shot his mouth off at the house. Surely the DEA would never dare use Ricky to force its will. Benito hoped desperately that he was right.

What was it Ricky had said when they argued here by the hangar yesterday? First he had called Benito a quitter for not stealing the airplane. But he had said something else. He'd said he wasn't a quitter himself. What had that meant? Was it just bluster?

How much had Ricky heard? Had he overheard where the León drug cartel kept the Skyhawk? It was possible— he seemed to have heard everything else. Benito did not like the fearful suspicion shadowing his thoughts. There had to be some other explanation.

Running toward the house, Benito sifted other possibilities through his mind. He had already wasted most of the day at home instead of searching. It bothered him how Ricky had implied that stealing the airplane would take care of his mother's death. How had Ricky put it?

If you didn't take care of a wound, it got infected? Benito tried not to be angry. That's how boys thought.

Back in Ricky's room Benito rummaged through every drawer—something might give him a clue. Next he turned to the closet. Inside the bifold door sat Ricky's neatly stacked gym clothes and his good gym sneakers. Benito bent and picked up the sneakers. If Ricky's clothes were here, what was in the bag he took to school? It had been full.

He tried to put himself in Ricky's place. What would he do? The answer made him swallow. He'd want desperately to get back at those responsible. That had been Benito's reaction three years ago, but he hadn't dared do anything for fear they would hurt Ricky. Now a hollow, sick feeling churned in the pit of his gut.

If Ricky thought he could go get the plane, he would have needed money for bus fares. Benito rushed to the hallway and opened the storage closet where he kept the stash of Mexican pesos. Quickly he pulled down the old shoe box and flipped up the cover. Empty!

"Oh, *mi 'jito*," he muttered. Then he blessed himself. *"Madre de Cristo! Madre de Dios!"* His son had no idea who he was dealing with. Drug smugglers weren't members of the human race. Their greed made them brutal and vicious.

Making matters worse, if Ricky had gone after the plane, this would have to be handled outside of regular channels. A normal runaway could be searched for by the police. They would send out an all-points bulletin. But the police had little authority across the border. Considering the presidential summit, the confidential signature radar, and the DEA's efforts to steal a plane on foreign soil, local authorities might blunder in and get Ricky killed. No, the DEA was responsible. If Ricky had gone to Mexico, then the DEA would get him out. Or else!

Benito picked up the phone and dialed. It took several minutes for a secretary to connect him with Frank Page, his old boss. Frank listened patiently but made it clear that he doubted Ricky was in fact after the plane. Benito couldn't blame the man—he didn't know Ricky's spunk. And Frank probably feared the horrible implications.

"Stay near your phone," Frank Page said. "I'll call you after I check this out."

"Yeah. Check it out better than you did my wife's accident," Benito snapped angrily. "Remember, this time your neck's on the block." He slammed down the phone. Immediately he felt ashamed for letting his anger flare.

He waited. Fifteen minutes later Frank Page called back. "Benito," he asked, "can you come in immediately for a priority meeting?"

"On my way."

"Oh, one more thing. Bring several pictures of Ricky."

"Done!" Benito hung up. In record time he swerved the pickup out the drive and headed toward town. When he arrived at the sprawling brick DEA complex, Frank Page greeted him. All else aside, the man was a good director, well intentioned, although a little too much by the book. The joke going around the agency when Benito worked there was that Frank Page got dressed each morning with the help of an operations manual. Listening to him now, Benito realized nothing had changed.

"Come in," Frank said, holding open the door to the conference room. "I hope we can resolve this matter."

Benito held out Ricky's pictures. "Resolve this matter?" he said. "Is that what you call finding a missing boy?" He wanted to shake the man and tell him that Ricky wasn't simply a matter that needed resolving. He was a real live child, a son, in more danger than anyone imagined.

Ignoring Benito's outburst, Frank Page glanced at the pictures. Also in the room sat two agents, Dexter Crumm and Buck Winslow—the same ones who visited the ranch with Frank. Benito liked Buck. The tall quiet Montanan was a hard worker and knew when not to talk. Dexter Crumm was a whole different story. He would get into a hundred-mile-per-hour chase to issue a parking ticket. He was a bald, tired-looking man.

Both men had been regular agents when Benito worked the agency. Now they worked Special Affairs Division. It explained how Dexter had gotten so cocky— "badge heavy," they called it in the agency. Someday it would get him into trouble.

"Benito," Frank Page started in. "Have a seat. Based on what you told me over the phone, and with what's at stake, I called the State Department. I let them know about Ricky. Needless to say, they're nervous as chickens in a snake pit."

Dexter Crumm spoke up, looking directly at Benito. "I think you're dreaming—blowing this whole thing out of shape. Your kid is probably down playing video games at the mall. A boy his age would hardly care about stealing an airplane. He wouldn't dare go after it unless he's dumber than we think. And suppose he did, he'd never get within a mile of the Skyhawk. Can he even fly that kind of plane?"

The man's tone of voice irritated Benito. He met the agent's dour stare. "Dexter," he said thickly, "Ricky could fly a Skyhawk upside down under your chin. I don't know about your kid, but mine has learned to do more than play video games. Yesterday Ricky tried his first solo loop in our Baby Great Lakes biplane."

Dexter Crumm turned red. "Your boy is violating the law flying solo at his age. You think that just because—"

"Easy now!" Frank Page interrupted. "It doesn't matter if Ricky could actually steal the plane—I think we all agree that would be quite impossible. But if he were to get caught trying, he could expose our involvement. That would leave the president with egg on his face. We can't chance that."

Frank Page was probably right about not being able to steal the plane, Benito thought. But to dismiss his son so lightly irked him. Ricky had his faults. He was hotheaded, stubborn, and prone to shortcuts. Not so very unlike his father, Benito admitted. But Ricky also had more nerve and gravel in his craw than these men imagined. His shy nature covered up a whole lot.

"I want you both on this full time," Frank Page said, handing a picture of Ricky to each agent. "Don't come up for air until Ricky Díaz is found. Understand?"

Buck Winslow nodded obediently.

Dexter Crumm grumbled his agreement.

"Benito, I know this is your son," Frank Page continued. "But I'm going to ask that you sit this one out. This is a DEA operation, and I'm playing it by the book. We'll do everything possible to find Ricky, and I'll keep you informed of our progress. Okay?"

Benito nodded. He knew the game—it had been his life for more years than he cared to admit. He also knew that his nod meant little. If there was something he thought would help find Ricky, all the badges in Arizona wouldn't keep him home.

"One more thing! Because the State Department is involved and because of the sensitive nature, I want this whole thing kept under wraps. We're dealing with a small boy who is a flier, so I'm code-naming this 'Operation Sparrow Hawk.' I can't stress enough the sensitive nature of this matter. Any communication or reference to the operation will be under that code name. Understood?"

Dexter shifted his massive bulk in the chair and let out a snort of disdain.

"Go ahead and check out his friends, police reports, and local hangouts," Frank added. "But to be safe, we must initially operate on the assumption that Ricky is already in Mexico and attempting to acquire the plane. So, effective immediately, gentlemen, Operation Sparrow Hawk is alert level green. Now, on the long chance that young Ricky makes it into the drug compound, we will upgrade that to alert level orange. At that point, I'm afraid the State Department will have to get directly involved."

"What if he gets the plane in the air?" Benito asked.

Frank Page started picking up his papers as if the meeting were concluded. "Oh, I don't think we ever have to worry about this going code red!"

7

Ricky felt invisible. What had he done to himself? Everything that made him Ricky Díaz was gone—his good clothes, his ID, his long hair, everything! All he had left was his dark skin and clothes his mother would have torn up for rags. The dusty ditch into Mariposa grew long. Cars sped past, nobody even glancing at him. Ricky tried to spit but choked on his tears. Something deep inside screamed, "I'm Ricky Díaz. Please look at me, I'm me! I exist!"

Mom's murder had turned the world upside down. Would she have recognized him right now? He tried talking to her. "I don't care what happens," he muttered. "I'll get the airplane. They shouldn't have killed you, Mamá."

Today she didn't answer.

Stubborn questions needled Ricky as he walked. What would Dad do this afternoon when the school bus didn't stop at the ranch? What if there was no Skyhawk at the drug compound? Would he get caught? Thinking made Ricky's head hurt, and he concentrated instead on kicking rocks down the littered ditch.

He squinted his eyes against the afternoon sun and yawned. Sleep was catching up to him. Maybe he'd find a place to stay tonight and try to get at the plane in the morning. It would be dumb to steal the plane, then fall asleep trying to fly it home. Also he'd grown hungry.

On the edge of town small adobe houses baked in the afternoon sun. Faded pink, blue, and red stucco crumbled in patches from their low walls. The air felt lazy. A small, mangy dog barked indifferently. Housewives worked the backyards, stringing out and taking in wash from the clothesline. Several had young children clinging to their long dresses.

One lady watched him approach and called her young boy in from the street where he'd been playing with marbles. She held the boy tightly to her side until Ricky had passed. Farther along, another lady yelled at him in Spanish, "Leave the chickens alone!" Ricky looked ahead and spotted several chickens strutting and pecking along the gutter. He walked wide around them. What did she think he was going to do, steal a chicken? Ricky had to smile to himself. At least his disguise was getting some reaction.

Mariposa hadn't seemed this big the last time he'd been down here with his father. For ten blocks Ricky walked through cluttered neighborhoods before reaching the busy downtown stores and shops. Off on a side street, a guitar and accordion sent lively *ranchera* music echoing through the air—also laughter and shouting. The festivity lifted Ricky's spirits, and he hummed to himself. A big, juicy burrito would sure taste good.

Down the block he spotted a food stand, actually a big cart with bicycle tires at one end. A squat lady watched him approach. She worked deftly, turning roasted corn and stirring fried meat. Her Santa Claus belly formed a table on which she rested her huge, flabby arms. It was obvious where some of her tacos and burritos ended up. Ricky looked at the sizzling meat chunks, and his mouth watered.

Four older boys watched idly from a nearby bench, joking and shoving at each other. Ricky wondered why they weren't in school. Impatiently he ordered a couple of burritos.

"*Puedes pagar?*" said the lady, asking if he could pay. He let his irritation show. "*Sí!*"

"*A ver.*" She extended her hand.

Ricky couldn't believe it. He'd like to dive-bomb her tortilla cart with the biplane. Nobody had ever questioned whether he could pay for food before. Cripes, this was a couple of burritos, not a gold watch! Brazenly he pulled the wad of bills from his pocket and waved them in her face. "Think this is enough?" He spoke in Spanish.

The lady eyed him curiously. Behind, on the bench, the laughing and joking stopped. Quickly Ricky peeled off two bills and stuffed the rest in his pocket. Why did he have to be so stupid? Considering the grubby clothes, was it any wonder the lady thought him penniless—or *peso*less?

Burritos in hand, he hurried away. Every time Dad brought him to Mexico, they ate themselves sick on tortillas, tacos, roasted corn, enchiladas, and burritos. According to Dad, no other place on earth had tortillas this fresh off the stove and salsa guaranteed to melt your socks.

Ricky paused and took a bite of the spicy burrito, at the same time glancing around. The four boys near the food stand were on their feet and following him. Ricky picked up his walk. The boys broke into a run. Ricky knew he couldn't outrun them, and this sure wasn't the Mariposa Welcome Wagon committee, so he ducked inside a small leather-clothes shop.

The shopkeeper met him with a severe look. *"Vete!"* he shouted, pointing back out the door.

Ricky stammered, trying to explain. But the man grabbed him roughly by the shirt and spun him around. *"Vete!"* he yelled, shoving hard and waving his arm. The approaching boys drew up short, waiting like wolves for the shopkeeper to turn his back.

Ricky saw the boys' impatient and crooked grins. "You want these," he hollered. "Take them!" He pitched his juicy burritos at the clustered group, scoring a sloppy bull's-eye. Before they could react, he sprinted down the street. The boys gave chase, their footsteps pounding loud.

Ricky dashed across the street and into an empty alley. Frantically he searched for someplace to hide. Tall brick walls lined both sides. Only the far end allowed any escape. Behind, the pursuing footsteps echoed hollow as they came onto gravel. They drew closer. A look back surprised Ricky. Only two boys remained in pursuit. If half had already given up, they weren't as tough as they looked.

A loud horn blasted. Ahead a big dump truck swung into the alley from the far street. It lumbered toward Ricky, engine growling. The sides of the huge machine nearly touched the brick walls. Ricky knew he could never slide past without getting hit.

The two boys closed in quickly, mean, hungry looks on their faces. Sight of the truck did not slow them. The truck blasted its horn again. The driver kept up his speed, shaking a fist. He yelled something out the window.

Ricky ran directly at the truck. Surprise showed in the driver's eyes, and loud air brakes screeched. Again the horn blared urgently. At the last second, when he was sure to be hit, Ricky slid to his back as if he were stealing a base. He lay flat as the truck roared over him. The axles and muffler brushed past with a deafening rumble. The skidding tires kicked sharp gravel. Ricky closed his eyes and imagined being crushed, his mangled body flopped over and over. The driver had probably not seen him drop.

The roar stopped, and Ricky opened one eye. Beautiful bright sunlight made him squint. The truck had jolted to a dusty stop only feet away. Lungs heaving, Ricky scrambled to his feet and kept running. Behind him the two boys had dropped to their stomachs and were squirming under the long truck.

"*Cabrón!*" swore the driver, bellowing like a bull and shaking his fist out the window. He could not open his door because of the narrow alley.

The boys kept wiggling in the dirt. Ricky ran, sure now of his escape. Another few seconds and he'd be back on the busy street. He slowed to catch his breath.

Suddenly the other two missing boys rounded the corner into the alley ahead of Ricky. They had flanked him! Behind, the first two slithered out from under the truck's bumper and jumped to their feet. The truck revved its engine impatiently and rumbled away. Ricky swallowed and drew up short. As Dad would say, things were getting inconvenient. Soon the fight would be against four, not two.

Without waiting, Ricky dashed straight at the boys nearest the street. They stopped, surprised, then braced for his charge. He swerved purposely into the tallest Mexican. The collision knocked the large boy down with a surprised grunt. Ricky stumbled but kept his footing. The other boy grabbed his shirt from behind. He turned and struck hard, hitting a chin.

The boy grunted, swearing to kill Ricky. *"Te mataré!"* he yelped, punching back. His fist caught Ricky's neck, stunning him. Ricky flailed his arms in circles. These boys might get his money, but they'd have to earn it. Let them try attacking a windmill.

The first boy scrambled back to his feet and circled behind. *"Dame la lama,"* he ordered, holding out his hand. *"Dámelo!"* The other boys were fast approaching.

"If you want the money, take it from me," Ricky muttered in English. He lashed out, striking the boy in the stomach. The lanky kid bent at the waist, coughing. The other boy backed away and circled like a wolf.

"Dame la lama," he repeated with a growl, holding out his hand.

Against two, it had figured to be a good fight. But the others arrived on the run. With no caution, they plunged straight into Ricky's flailing fists. One shoved hard, knocking Ricky to the ground. The rest gang-piled on top and started punching.

Ricky struggled, but strong hands gripped his arms. Someone sat on his stomach and reached into his pockets. With a satisfied laugh, the boy pulled out the money and jackknife.

"You jerks!" Ricky screamed, bucking hard and twisting to throw off his attackers. But they pinned him tightly. The only thing Ricky could do was kick, so kick he did. Over and over he struck out with his feet, bringing a barrage of punches each time he connected.

The tallest boy kneeled on Ricky's head and scraped his cheek sideways in the dirt. His bare foot pushed into Ricky's face. Spitting out gravel, Ricky twisted and lunged, biting squarely into a big toe. The boy howled desperately, cussing and swearing. Ricky bit harder. His attacker fell into the dirt screaming, then rolled and kicked Ricky in the face.

The alley spun in darkness. Fists kept clobbering him, but the punches grew distant and vague, as in a dream. A faint siren wailed, growing louder. The beating stopped. The air, so filled with noise, grew silent, except for the siren. Then it, too, stopped. Ricky struggled to breathe into the wavering darkness. His head roared, his thoughts drifted. If pilots ever blacked out and lost control in an airplane, bad things happened. That was probably true of alley fights, too. A fog of light crept back into Ricky's vision, much like coming out of a loop. Still everything remained silent and unmoving.

When the darkness cleared, he sat up. One eye puffed nearly closed, and he tasted blood. Again and again he coughed and swallowed. His senses returned, and with it waves of pain crashed in. Lips and cheeks felt numb, as if he were coming from the dentist. His legs and ribs felt as if the truck had run over him. The world seemed to swirl and rock unsteadily. Every breath hurt.

Ricky blinked back hot tears of anger. His mouth was too sore to spit. If ever he met any of these boys alone, he'd . . . he'd . . . Again he swallowed. He noticed his feet and saw that they were bare. Those jerks had taken his tennis shoes, too.

"Thieves! Dirty, rotten thieves!" Ricky muttered bitterly. All he had left was the ragged shirt and pants he wore. Awkwardly he struggled to stand. The ground swayed, and his gut churned. The four boys had disappeared, but still Ricky sensed someone watching. Maybe the boys were waiting to do a little more pounding.

He hobbled toward the street, pressing one hand against his ribs. The gravel stung his feet. Why did they have to take his shoes? Before getting beaten up, Ricky hadn't noticed the broken glass in the alley. Now he tiptoed to avoid it. Out on the street, many people were walking barefoot. They didn't seem to mind.

Again he had the sense that someone was watching. Ricky turned quickly and glimpsed a person ducking behind a sidewalk display of tourist knickknacks, someone short and dark. Ricky looked straight ahead and kept walking. He didn't mind someone watching him, but he didn't like being followed. And this person was shadowing him. Stalking him.

Ricky tried to ignore his follower. All he wanted to do was go home. But not before finding the boys who had beaten him up—he'd find them one at a time. First he needed sleep and he needed food. His thoughts grew confused. At home these problems were simple. The refrigerator held ham and cheese for sandwiches, cookies, pop, and anything else he wanted. He dreamed of a bathtub full of hot water. It could soak away all this dirt and grime—in fact, it could wash away this whole terrible nightmare. He dreamed also of sleeping in a soft, clean bed. His water bed.

This whole situation stank!

Ricky watched several scrawny, half-naked boys huddled on the curb of the sidewalk next to a light post. They stared vacantly into space, dazed, unaware of anything around them. One boy slept, his legs hanging out into the street, feet half submerged in murky gutter water. Dad would not call these boys *rateros*. He'd say they were homeless or less fortunate children. Ricky could not see how they were anything but *rateros*. Street rats! Gingerly he headed down the sidewalk to look for a better place to sleep. He was Ricky Díaz, not a *ratero*.

Again the dark-faced person appeared, peeking over a parked car on the opposite side of the street. For a second Ricky found himself looking into the eyes of a young girl.

Again Ricky lost sight of her on the crowded sidewalk. He hated being stalked, even by a girl. Sluggishly he turned and ran after her. Each step shot pain through his tender feet and ankles, quickly forcing him to hobble to a stop. A lame turtle could outrun him, Ricky thought. Why did the jerks have to take his shoes? The street and sidewalk seemed to waver, and his body grew heavy. Had the beating caused this? Maybe it was from not having slept the night before.

His brain felt numb. Shaking his head didn't help. Thoughts of the ranch, of Mom, of Dad, of the Baby Great Lakes biplane, pressed in on him. His life in Arizona seemed so distant, almost from another world. He felt lost. Somehow he had to find food, but how?

Ricky scanned the ground. Maybe he could find some money. People often dropped change on sidewalks or in parking lots. Here it ought to be easy, considering all the litter. Gingerly he limped forward on the edges of his feet, clenching his teeth against the pain.

Two blocks of searching left him grimacing and frustrated. No wonder he couldn't find anything. Around him a dozen beggars and *rateros* scrounged, rummaging through the trash cans and gutters. One group was a family—a mother, a father, and two very young girls. Most of what they found ended up in their mouths. Farther down the block, a young boy, maybe seven years old, ran over and grabbed a piece of old gum from the gutter. He stuffed it into his mouth and chewed hungrily. Ricky shuddered.

Ahead a tall white *turista* and his wife approached. She wore a bright, long dress and shiny shoes as if she had dressed up to come here. He wore baggy white pants and a shirt with big pineapples painted on the front. The couple spoke loudly, acting unaware of the many eyes that watched them.

A cluster of *rateros* shadowed them from a safe distance, their hands extended. In broken English, they pleaded, "Please, señor. Please, señora." Ricky pushed past the *rateros* and stepped in front of the husband and wife. The big man broke stride to avoid colliding. Ricky spoke in English. "Excuse me, sir."

They appeared surprised. The husband stared with piercing eyes, then laughed openly. "That's cute. You've learned English real well—swindling tourists."

Ricky extended his hand. "I'm from Arizona," he said. "Please, mister, can I have some money for food?" He didn't dare explain how he'd come to be in Mariposa.

The towering man waved his arm. "Right! And I'm from Mars. Go get a job."

The blond wife adjusted her huge green sunglasses. "Let's go, honey," she said impatiently.

Ricky kept his hand outstretched. "Just a little bit?" he begged, pleading with his eyes.

"Is your hearing bad?" the man growled. Then he forced a smile. "Oh, okay. Here, maybe something little." He dug into his pocket and held out his clenched hand.

Eagerly Ricky reached up.

With a hoarse laugh, the man dropped an empty gum wrapper. "Is that little enough? Now, get!" He barged forward, bumping Ricky aside.

Ricky threw the crumpled wrapper angrily at the man. The motion caught the big tourist's eye, and he spun around. With his bear-paw hand he cuffed Ricky on the shoulder and knocked him down. "Try that again, I'll wring your neck," he snarled. The wife grabbed her husband's hand and towed him away.

Ricky cowered as the couple's loud talk faded. Finally he stood. The group of *rateros* had gathered in a half circle, giggling. Ricky avoided their stares and retreated down the sidewalk. This time he did not notice the small, curious eyes still following him from the opposite side of the street.

He'd sure gotten into a mess. His stomach pinched with hunger. He winced as each step drove pain up his legs. He wanted to go home, but he could barely walk. An inner voice kept coaxing him to not give up, to keep looking for the plane. Ricky hobbled on, hungry and tired. He couldn't go after the plane in this condition.

The bright sun made the sidewalk hot as a frying pan. Even walking in the shade, pain pulsed in his legs, keeping time with his heartbeat. His jaw ached with a dull throbbing. Ricky balanced on one leg and examined his sorest foot. Blood seeped from the red and puffy heel.

Ricky clenched his teeth and limped into the nearest alley, drawn by the sight of several discarded cardboard boxes. The sharp gravel bit at his feet like burning matches. Dropping to his hands and knees, he crawled into the largest box. Now both feet were oozing blood. He had to pinch his eyes closed to keep from crying out.

A scratchy noise brought his eyes open. Two feet away, a fat gray rat nosed forward and scurried out and across the alley. Heart pounding, Ricky groaned and collapsed back. Life had become a nightmare. His body seemed to float through space. What time was it—maybe late afternoon? Tomorrow he would get out of here. Now, though, nothing mattered more than sleep. He had to sleep. It was all he could think of, and slowly he relaxed.

Down he drifted, deeper and deeper. Once he jerked awake, thinking he felt the rat crawling across his body. He brushed his hands sharply over his chest. Nothing was there. The alley lay silent in the afternoon sun. Ricky shifted positions, but more sharp gravel poked up through the cardboard. He imagined lying on his big, soft water bed at home. Why had it never seemed special before? Again he relaxed and slept. And he dreamed.

At home, dreams were always about planes and pilots and astronauts. Here the very air was different. Sights, sounds, people, their food, their language—everything had a different feel and flavor. Weird thoughts and images had come to him from nowhere. He had started thinking and understanding differently. And when he slept he dreamed of new things. But they did not seem new.

He dreamed he was a *ratero,* standing at the head of a long parade of people. The people were in groups and stretched to the horizon. They came from other places and other times. Aztecs. Mayans. There were Mixtecs and Toltecs. Olmecs and Zapotecs. Beyond them wound miles of soldiers and kings and queens and horses, and beyond them mothers with children, and grandparents. Some Ricky recognized; Montezuma and Zapata. He spotted his parents and grandparents. He even waved to them, but they did not see him. There were millions he did not recognize. Even cavemen. But they all followed and watched carefully to see where he would lead them. Ricky felt important. He felt responsible. And scared. *Rateros* should not lead parades.

How long he slept he did not know.

The sound of gravel grating outside the box snapped him awake. He listened. Only silence. Hard yawns would not drive the numbing weariness away. He blinked and sat up. Dusk had dimmed the alley. The big rat probably wanted the box back. Ricky peeked out.

A young girl sat cross-legged in the alley, facing him. Her frayed and baggy dress did not cover her thin, scabby knees. She smiled a nervous, crooked-toothed smile and scraped her bare toes back and forth in the dirt. Some of her teeth were missing. Her age was hard to tell because a flat nose, puffy cheeks, and big ears made her look odd. Tangled black hair hung to her shoulders. Several strands dangled over her curious dark eyes.

Ricky frowned. If she planned on robbing him while he slept, the joke was on her—dry turnips weren't worth squeezing. Then he recognized her and sat up. "You're the one who's been following me!" he said in Spanish.

She held up a small finger to her pudgy lips. "Shhhhh—it's okay. Go to sleep, I'll watch you." Her voice was hushed, her smile stubborn.

"Get out of here!" Ricky said.

"After you sleep."

Ricky regarded her for a long moment, then flopped backward. He closed his eyes, too tired to argue or worry.

A ten-foot rat with teeth the size of shovels bit down on Ricky's legs. It shook him back and forth, slaver whipping from its mouth. Bones crunched. Blood squirted and splashed in the dirt.

Ricky woke from his wild dream, breathing hard. It took a few seconds for the huge rat to retreat from his thoughts. Nothing made sense—the dark alley, the cold night, the cardboard box. He shivered, his torn blue jeans and ragged T-shirt doing little to ward off the cold night. It helped to roll onto his side and hug his knees to his chest. But still his teeth chattered. He could not see the moon, but the alley glowed in a dim wash of pale light.

He remembered the odd-looking girl and peeked out, searching the shadows. He was alone. A dark mound rested near the box. Cautiously he ventured out. In the dim moonlight Ricky found a plastic bottle, two dried and stiff tortillas, and a serape—a blanket with a head hole cut in the middle.

The *ratera* must have left this stuff, but why? Hands shaking, Ricky set the offerings inside the box. He stretched the serape over his head. The old and patched blanket stank like a dead animal, but it helped soften the cold. Still shivering, Ricky gulped from the plastic bottle. The foul-tasting water made him choke and sputter. He hoped it wouldn't make him sick. After swallowing two more stagnant mouthfuls, he sampled the dry tortillas. They could well have been used for Frisbees. He wasn't sure if the girl was trying to help him or kill him. Why had she done this?

It hurt to bite the dry dough. Splashing it with stale water helped but brought out a moldy taste. Ricky chewed and chewed. These things would clog a toilet! When he had forced down the last bite, he tugged the serape tighter and stood up to stretch. "Ouch!" he yelped, reminded of the pain in his feet. He collapsed, angrily, wondering if the boys from the alley fight hurt half this bad. With grim satisfaction he remembered the one whose toe he'd bitten.

Also memories of home teased his thoughts and brought with them even more anger. What was Dad doing, and why had he become a quitter? Ever since Mom had died, Ricky had been angry. Not directly at Dad but at the whole world. No one understood how he felt. Dad happened to be part of that world, and the more he tried to make things right, the more Ricky resented it. Things weren't right!

There were times, though, like right now, when Ricky wished he could talk to Dad about all that had happened. But he didn't dare, even if he could. Ricky had loved Mom. And when he lost her, it hurt too much. He decided to quit letting his feelings show. By guarding them, he would never let himself be hurt again. Not this bad.

Never ever again would he be anybody's wingman, or let anybody be his!

Ricky woke to her silent gaze. In the brisk dawn air, she sat across the alley, picking idly at her fingernails. She regarded him with big, curious eyes. Ricky scowled and sat upright. For the first time the light allowed a good look at this *ratera* who had followed him.

She wore only a bleached flour sack with a length of twine snugged tightly at the waist. Her skinny arms and neck poked out through ragged holes, and her thick hair hung in matted strands. Scars crossed her arms and legs—strange scars, parallel to each other.

Ricky squinted hard. "Who are you?" he queried in Spanish.

She did not answer but instead grinned boldly, seemingly proud of herself. This bothered Ricky. What was there to be proud of? He examined her more closely. Her fingernails were cracked and broken. A fresh pink thistle bloom gleamed in her black hair.

"Who are you?" Ricky demanded again.

She became suddenly bashful, looking down and fingering her pudgy nose. "Soledad," she offered, her voice barely a whisper. Then she peeked up with an impish smile.

Ricky couldn't be mad. But still he eyed her cautiously. Her name, Soledad, meant "solitude," or "alone."

"And who are you?" she whispered.

"Ricardo." Ricky used his Spanish name.

She looked quizzically at him, then blurted, "You don't look so good. Someone really screwed up your hair."

"*I* look bad!"

She nodded, smiling. "*Sí.*"

Ricky sat speechless. Arguing with a *ratera* over looks seemed pointless. The morning sun broke above the buildings, touching the air with warmth. Ricky peeled off the itchy serape and folded it, handing it to Soledad. "Thanks. And thanks for the food."

"The food was good! No?"

Ricky nodded. Good for gopher bait, he thought.

She glowed with self-importance.

Stiffly he stood and took a step. The sharp gravel bit into his feet. With a moan he dropped to the ground and grabbed his toes.

Soledad scrambled up. "You have gringo feet," she said. "Wait here."

Before Ricky could argue, she took off running. Her bowlegged gait swayed her like a windup toy. The gravel and glass didn't bother her as she bobbed out of sight. Who was this crazy girl? And why was she helping? Gingerly Ricky rubbed his sore ribs.

A twinge of pain, oddly enough, caused him to chuckle. He'd taken a beating all right, but it could have been worse. And somewhere in Mariposa four boys were waking up less than chipper, of this he was sure. Dad would have been proud. Or maybe not. Dad didn't like him to fight. He always said that it took a bigger person to stay out of a fight than to get into one. This was one time Ricky wished he really had been a bigger person so he could have really thumped the bums.

In minutes Soledad returned. She reached inside the neck of her flour-sack dress. "Look!" she said, huffing to catch her breath. "Huaraches!" She tossed a chunk of car tire on the ground. Next she pulled out a strip of inner tube, a rusty spike, and an old knife wrapped in a rag.

Ricky eyed her. Huaraches were sandals. But what was all this other junk?

She dropped to her knees and reached for his ankle. "Give me your foot," she said, pressing the tire tread against the bottom of his foot and tracing out its pattern with the rusty nail. Using the old knife, she began hacking away at the thick rubber, her hands moving with intensity. Her chin jutted forward as she worked.

Ricky watched. Whenever the thick rubber resisted, Soledad pursed her lips in concentration, gripped the knife harder, and attacked it. When her weary hands started to fumble, Ricky reached over and gently took hold of the knife and the rubber chunk. She conceded with a shy smile.

As Ricky worked, she eyed him. Suddenly she crossed

the alley. There she squatted with her back to him. A puddle formed and flowed from between her ankles. Ricky turned his head away. Soon she returned, watching him work as if nothing had happened.

"Why don't you go find a bathroom?" he said accusingly.

Soledad shrugged. "I don't want a bath." She looked at him quizzically. "Do you always use a bathroom?"

Ricky shook his head without answering. After he finished one sole, Soledad took it from him and twisted at it with the rusty spike, her tongue bunched between her lips. Every few minutes she glanced up, flashing openmouthed smiles.

Ricky watched the odd girl with fascination while she bored holes into the makeshift sandal. He traced out the other foot and began carving. He felt weak, and his stomach knotted tighter and tighter. It was no wonder. Since yesterday's breakfast at home, he'd only eaten one bite of a burrito and two dried tortillas. Gripping the knife became harder.

When both sandals were ready, Soledad shaved off narrow strips of inner tube to make laces and then fed them through the holes. Deftly she knotted the ends. With the thongs drawn tight, she proudly presented the finished product. "Here. These are good for gringo feet."

Ricky fitted the sandals to his feet, then stood, taking tentative steps. He had always thought huaraches were fine leather sandals. Who'd have ever thought to use old tires? His feet were still tender, but compared to walking barefoot, the sandals felt like pillows.

"Thanks a lot," he said sincerely.

She nodded. "Your Spanish sounds different. Where are you from?"

Ricky ignored the question. "Soledad," he asked, "where is the Camacho cattle ranch?"

"You mean Rancho Camacho?"

"I guess."

Fear and distrust clouded her face. "Why do you want to know?"

"I'm going to visit them."

"No! Don't go to that place. There's lots of bad hombres there."

"How do you know?"

"Everybody in Mariposa knows. Where are you from?"

"I need to know where it is," he said.

She eyed him suspiciously as she pointed. "It's five kilometers that way, on the road to San Vicente. But they have *bandidos* with big guns. You shouldn't go."

Ricky noticed her fearful eyes. "I have to," he said.

"Nothing is so important that you have to go to Rancho Camacho," she argued. As if the matter were settled, she changed the subject. "Are you hungry?" she asked.

"I'm starved. Do you know where there's food?"

She smiled broadly, puffing up her flat chest like a bird on a branch. "*Sí*, follow me." Turning, she scrambled off down the alley.

Ricky chased awkwardly after her, his big sandals flopping. Soledad charged ahead, her chin jutted forward. Ricky couldn't believe he was chasing after her. If only he weren't so hungry. "Hey! Wait for me," he shouted.

She stopped and turned.

When he caught up, he glanced about, embarrassed to be seen with the grubby little girl. But people passed them by on the street, hardly noticing. Ricky saw his reflection in a store window and his embarrassment deepened. He did not recognize himself. Not until he smiled and made a funny face did the image look familiar. He had not wanted to be recognized. But this bothered him. Here he felt invisible, like a piece of dirt on the street.

"Do you like good food?" Soledad asked. She started out again.

"Of course," Ricky said, following. "Why?"

She answered by angling across the street. A large new car raced toward her, blaring its horn. She walked slower, forcing the car to swerve abruptly. A smug smile creased her lips. As it passed she turned and stuck out her tongue.

Ahead the thrum of Spanish guitar floated from inside a fancy restaurant. A trumpet sounded clear through the air. Blinking lights surrounded a huge sign over the arched doorway. Restaurante del Sol.

"We'll eat here," Soledad announced.

Ricky stared in disbelief as Soledad passed by the front door and continued around the side of the building to the back door. She walked directly toward two garbage cans swarming with flies.

"You can have that one," she said, pointing to the fullest can.

Ricky stared at the can and at Soledad in numbed silence. Already she had started burrowing through her can, stuffing chunks and bits into her mouth. She glanced up briefly. "Hurry," she exclaimed, "or he'll catch us!"

10

Ricky balked.

"Hurry!" Soledad called, cramming her mouth with a handful of taco makings.

Still Ricky could not move. This was madness! Absolute insanity. The game had gone too far. But then he shook his head and took a deep breath. Mom's dying wasn't a game. It had never been a game. Nor was the beating he took in the alley yesterday. This hunger that chewed at his belly was anything but a game.

He wrinkled his nose at the dead smell of rotted food. Soledad used both hands to stuff handfuls of food into her mouth. Her ruddy cheeks bunched full like those of a pocket gopher. Reluctantly Ricky poked through his can. Under some paper and cardboard, he uncovered a glob of refried beans. His hand shook as he dipped two fingers in and scooped the mash to his tongue. It didn't taste all that bad. Hunger took over. Ricky shoveled up a whole handful and wolfed it down.

Next he dug out three half-eaten chicken wings. Without thinking, he wiped them off on his jeans, then gnawed at each. Again he glanced at Soledad. She hung half in, half out of her can, ejecting bits of trash over her shoulders. Ricky found most of an enchilada buried in cigarette ashes. This he couldn't handle. Underneath were two crushed bananas with black shriveled skins. They peeled easy, and he gulped down the brown mushy insides. Still chewing, he burrowed deeper.

"Quítate!" bellowed a gruff voice from very near. Ricky came up so fast that his head hit the can. He had not heard the back door open, but the booming voice shouting "Get out" took away his breath. Not ten feet away a massive man in a white chef's uniform brandished a shiny butcher knife. Ricky froze as if touched by an electric fence.

"Corre! Corre!" screamed Soledad.

Her voice snapped Ricky loose. He obeyed and ran after her. Ahead she stopped. He looked back. The chef stood wheezing near a light post, swearing. Soledad grabbed up a rock and pitched it sharply, barely missing the big man.

"Now he'll chase us," she said with a smile, her eyes sparkling.

Sure enough. The knife-waving chef ambled after them, his barrel stomach swaying like Jell-O. His footsteps pounded on the street.

Ricky took off running, his clumsy huaraches flopping. He looked back.

Soledad stood in place, clapping her hands. *"Bueno! Bueno!"* she screamed. When the man was nearly on her, she ducked, then ran, weaving left and right to keep him off balance. The whole thing reminded Ricky of a hippo chasing a squirrel. Soledad bounced and darted as she ran, her bony legs churning wildly. This was obviously not her first chase.

Quickly they outdistanced the chef. This relieved Ricky but set him to thinking. Part of him was angry—the guy had scared the innards out of him. And for what? Taking some garbage? Then another thought struck Ricky, and he laughed aloud. He'd heard of having to eat and run but never like this! It was Soledad's fault. She had thrown the rock, badgering the chef into chasing them. This knuckleheaded girl had helped him out, but now she was going to get him killed.

Wheezing, the chef kept lumbering after them. His knife glinted in the noon sun.

Ahead Ricky spotted other garbage cans set out for dumping. He slowed to encourage the chase.

"Rápido! Rápido!" Soledad screamed back.

As he approached the cans, Ricky slowed even more. He could hear the chef's rasping breath. The fat man closed the last ten feet and swung his knife in a whooshing arc. Ricky dodged and caught the edge of a full garbage can. He tipped it into the path of the raging chef.

A tremendous collision shattered the air. Then a solid thud and a loud grunt. The knife slid clanking against the curb. Soledad jumped up and down, laughing and clapping like a cheerleader—although Ricky had never seen a cheerleader who looked like her. *"Bravo! Bravo!"* she shouted as he rejoined her.

Ricky looked back. The big man lay sprawled on the street, his white uniform ripped and soiled. He writhed, clutching his knee, bellowing and cursing.

"I hope we didn't hurt him. Now maybe I'll have to throw two rocks so he'll chase me," Soledad said, sounding disappointed.

"Hope we didn't hurt him! Are you crazy? He was chasing us with a butcher knife! Has he chased you before?"

She nodded. "Sometimes he carries a bigger knife." She stretched her arms wide until they bent backward.

The chef struggled to one knee, a crazed look in his eyes. Still he kept hollering obscenities.

"He doesn't look happy," Soledad said. "Let's go."

Together they ran until the loud shouting faded away. When they stopped, Ricky turned to Soledad. "Why didn't you tell me he's chased you before?"

"It would ruin a good meal," she said with an impish grin, still panting from the chase.

"Good meal?" Ricky choked. "You didn't say anything about it being from a garbage can!"

She looked puzzled. "Where did you want to eat?" she asked. "At a table?" Her giggly laughter split the air. "You're weird, Ricardo." When she saw him not smiling, she frowned. Her large black eyes turned serious. "Don't be mad, we're amigos. No?"

Ricky couldn't avoid her pleading stare. "I guess we're friends," he answered. Still she looked hurt, so he added, "All right, thanks. Thanks for the food."

"You're very welcome," she said, bowing low. Her smile stretched nearly ear to ear.

Ricky thought of what he should do next. He wanted to go home. But without money and decent clothes, it would be nearly impossible to go back through the border. His original idea of going after the plane would be easier, and a lot faster.

"Listen," he said to Soledad. "I need to go to Rancho Camacho."

Again the fearful look stole into her eyes. "Why?"

"I can't tell you."

"No! Don't! I mean it," she said. "They have guns. This big!" Again she spread her skinny arms. "They'll kill you. You won't ever come back."

Soledad was half right, Ricky thought. He hoped he would never come back here. Ignoring her, he turned and started walking west toward the edge of the city.

Soledad trailed behind, eyeing him. She followed for a mile until they reached the open desert. Then she stopped. "Don't make them mad," she called. "I'll wait here."

Ricky turned. Her eager yet stubborn look left him feeling guilty. But why? He'd come to Mexico to get an airplane. Who was she to him? Telling her about the airplane would only cause troubles. Still he felt sad.

"I'll wait," she repeated with an imploring gaze.

Ricky turned away toward Rancho Camacho. In the distance thunder rumbled. To the south huge black clouds churned on the horizon. A light breeze was nudging at the clumps of tumbleweed. The prospect of bad weather hadn't bothered Ricky earlier. Now the air felt heavy and foreboding. He kicked at a clod of dirt with his bare toes and immediately regretted it. Nothing had gone right since he'd come to Mariposa.

He began to walk fast—and for more than one reason. After dropping over the first low hill, he slipped out behind a mesquite bush. He had to urinate. Soledad had been right. *Rateros* would be kicked out of any store or restaurant if they went inside to use the bathroom. But after criticizing her for how she'd relieved herself in the street, he didn't dare do the same thing. Instead he had clenched his teeth and curled his toes for two hours.

Finishing, Ricky continued on toward Rancho Camacho. His plan now was simple. First, he would go to the ranch, pretending he was looking for work. Then he would approach the Skyhawk as if curious. When no one was watching, he would crawl in. Suddenly Ricky thought of something. He no longer had his jackknife. If the keys weren't in the ignition, how could he cut and strip the ignition wires to get the plane running? Answering his own question, Ricky spotted a discarded tin can. He picked it up and twisted off the sharp bent-back cover. It would have to do. He hoped desperately that the ignition wiring was the same as the biplane's. And with luck the Skyhawk would be gassed up.

Ricky kept walking. This gravel road was not used heavily like the main highway entering Mariposa from the north. Only two cars drove past. The desert sun simmered high in the sky. A movement out among the mesquite caught Ricky's eye. A dusty kit fox trotted from behind a stand of barrel cactus dragging a long rattlesnake in its mouth. The miniature, fuzzy-haired fox glanced around nervously as flashes of lightning joined the thunder only miles away. Gray banks of rain hid the horizon.

The uncertainty of this flight haunted Ricky. Flights back home were all planned out. Sometimes a small airplane couldn't take off from a high desert strip on a hot day. The air wasn't dense enough to hold the weight. With the radar and a lot of fuel, the plane might be overweight. If only he could call the flight service station for a weather report. Even on clear days, high wind could bugger a flight. Today there was no access to such information, and a storm brewed to the south. He would be climbing into a strange, low-powered airplane with no preparation.

Ricky wished his father were here to help. Benito always seemed to know everything or have clever ideas up his sleeve. Again the thoughts of his father brought back feelings of anger and bitterness. If Dad had done what he should, if he hadn't been a quitter, none of this mess would have happened.

Ricky worried most about the Skyhawk. Was it kept in good condition by the drug smugglers? Or was it a heap of tin held together with chewing gum, baling wire, and shoestrings? What kind of runway was there for the takeoff run? Was there a wind sock? This whole thing was a blind turkey shoot!

Soledad had said Rancho Camacho was out five kilometers, or a little over three miles. Ricky figured he'd walked several kilometers already. He licked his finger and held it up, then tossed a handful of dust into the air and watched it drift. The light wind blew southward.

That meant a takeoff facing the north with the western sun on the left. There would be no time to puzzle over things like wind direction once the show started.

As he figured his plan, Ricky kicked a can down the littered ditch. Because his bare toes jutted from his home-made sandals, he side-kicked the can like a soccer ball. With each kick, he pretended to score a winning goal. A dozen buzzards lined the highway, perched boldly on fence posts. They croaked and clapped their big wings as Ricky passed. At Rancho Camacho there would be no pretending. Everything would be real: the people, the airplane, the danger. Deliberately Ricky kicked harder.

The gravel road climbed and dipped its way across the rolling desert, each rise blocking view of the next. As Ricky trudged up a long slope, he thought of Soledad. Something about that crazy girl had gotten to him. He hoped she would be okay. That notion struck him funny. She'd be just fine. She had taken care of herself—and him, too—since he'd shown up. He'd never admit it to her, however. She'd probably puff her chest up until it popped like a balloon.

Intently he kept going. Because of his kicking, and because of the rolling road, Ricky failed at first to notice the parked car. He looked up to find a new tan-colored car with U.S. license plates directly ahead and very near. The driver sat alone, watching him approach. Ricky had no choice but to keep walking. Deliberately he kept kicking the can. The driver watched him approach, then suddenly brought a camera up and snapped a picture.

Ricky swallowed at the lump in his throat. He recognized the thin DEA agent, one of the three who had visited the house. What was the man doing here? Heart pounding, Ricky kept walking. Nobody knew he was after the plane. How could they?

He quit kicking the can and avoided the agent's stare. It seemed unlikely that anyone would recognize him. He hadn't recognized himself in the store window. But what if they did? Just in case, he decided to play it safe. After dropping over the next rise, he cut from the road out to a dry river bottom nearby. The shoulder-deep arroyo angled in the direction of the Camacho ranch. If the agent followed, he would have to come on foot.

The southern sky grew darker as lightning flashed and crackled. Streaming curtains of rain hung from the distant clouds. Someone was getting a good *chubasco*, Ricky thought. He kept hiking the arroyo, staying out of sight until the riverbed curved to the north. At that point he considered crawling up the bank to be sure he was still headed toward Rancho Camacho. He had to keep heading westward. Although the sun burned brightly overhead, thunder kept rumbling and echoing in the distance.

A gravelly whisper touched the air. The sound grew louder, swiftly becoming a dull roar. Ricky paused in midstride. He looked back up the arroyo and froze. A three-foot wall of water gushed down the ravine directly at him, thundering like a stampede.

"The *chubasco*!" he gasped. The storm on the horizon had caused a flash flood here on dry ground! Ricky knew this could happen, but he hadn't considered it—he had been daydreaming about getting the plane.

Gravel shifted under the tumbling wall of water and sent out a grinding hiss. Tangles of shrub churned over and over in the tidal wave, like vegetables in a blender. The water seemed mad. Ricky raced toward the gravel edge of the arroyo and clawed his way up the dirt bank. Feet slipping, he lunged up and grabbed on to a gnarled bush. The water crashed past, swirling around his legs, splashing, threatening to suck him off the bank. Ricky hung on. Grunting and kicking, he pulled himself over the edge. The churning water splashed at him as he lay trembling.

The torrent raged past, spitting sharp spray high into the air. Ricky dared not move. He half expected the wall of water to come over the bank and chase him. Instead it boiled out of sight down the ravine, followed by a river of frothy water. The strong current flowed past for several minutes, then swirled lower, foaming as it re-treated. To the south the sky grew lighter, and the curtains of rain faded. Ricky watched and waited.

At last he crawled to his feet, trembling. Nothing hurt. His pants were soaked, but luckily he had not lost his sandals—Soledad's rubber thongs had held. Shallow blankets of bubbling murk covered the gully floor, leaving little trace of the *chubasco*.

Ricky stumbled to the highway. At first he turned toward Mariposa, but he stopped. Why should he return? He wasn't hurt. And now the weather looked better. Drawing in a deep breath, he headed back toward the drug compound.

Ahead a red clay side road branched off. Ricky looked around but could not spot the agent's car. Walking on the road made him a sitting duck, but memories of the *chubasco* scared him worse.

A small hand-painted sign was posted in the ground at the junction. It read Rancho Camacho. The sign made this look like an ordinary run-down ranch. Exactly what the drug dealers wanted, Ricky thought. He smiled. The alley fight, Soledad, the *chubasco*, everything had slowed him down. But now he was here. This was it!

The narrow, rutted driveway snaked off among low hills and ravines like a curling ribbon. Red-barked manzanita lined both sides. Walking was easy, but the sandals flopped and chafed Ricky's feet. He'd have given anything for some good thick socks and a pair of tennis shoes.

The road made a sharp bend. Rounding the corner, Ricky stopped and crouched. Within a stone's throw, he spotted an armed guard. The huge mule of a man cradled a machine gun loosely in one arm. His extra cartridges bristled in a loop around his broad belly. He leaned on a metal gate that barricaded the road. A tall fence, with rolled barbed wire on top, stretched away in both directions. The ranch looked like a prison.

Ricky ducked into the underbrush. Slowly he inched forward. Beyond the fence lay a large, shallow valley and a compound with nearly a dozen buildings. The guard had full view of everything. It would be impossible to sneak in during daylight.

Beyond the buildings stretched a small airstrip, cluttered with a surprising number of aircraft. Three Bell helicopters—looking like dragonflies—surrounded a large storage shed. Halfway down the runway a silver split-tailed Beechcraft glinted in the sun. Nearby was parked a newer twin-engine Piper. It looked like a Mojave or a Mirage. Out alone in a field sat a weathered old DC-3, tethered and abandoned, tires flat.

And then Ricky spotted it! All he could see was the nose cowling and prop of a small airplane, parked mostly inside the shed. But the dull orange-and-white paint was unmistakable.

Ricky trembled with giddy excitement. Now he had to get close to the plane, start it, and fly home. But first he would have to figure a way past the front gate. If he tried to crawl over the tall fence and rolled barbed wire, it would have to be at night. That meant hiding inside the drug compound until daybreak when he could see to take off. Ricky made up his mind. He crawled back over to the road, swallowed hard, and stood up. In plain view, he walked forward.

The guard stiffened when he saw the visitor. "*Qué quieres?*" he challenged in a deep, rumbling voice. His face looked mean as he demanded to know what Ricky wanted.

"I'm here to see if you need help," Ricky called back in Spanish from several hundred feet away. "I can take care of cows and sheep. I was—"

Before Ricky had finished speaking, the guard raised his machine gun. A loud burst of shots ripped the air, and flames leaped from the short barrel. Ricky jumped back, tripped, and fell hard. Gravel exploded as bullets raked the road.

The guard waved the gun menacingly. "Next time you come here," he rumbled in Spanish, "I'll kill you!"

12

Instantly Ricky was back on his feet, running for his life. The guard's coarse voice and the sharp ricocheting echo of gunshots drove Ricky with a hollow terror. Down the long road he raced, stumbling, until the guard's hacking laughter slowly faded away. He kept running.

Beside the main road he staggered to a stop. Pain stung his chest and sides. He gasped, bending to catch his breath. Everything blurred and tilted. His legs trembled. Ricky squinted back toward Rancho Camacho. Those jerks had killed his mom. He steadied himself with a long, deep breath. He had to reach the plane. He just had to! Fists clenched, he stood upright and headed back toward Mariposa.

Ricky wanted to avoid the agent's car, but memory of the *chubasco* kept him near the road. The water had growled like a monster that wanted to kill. He kept to

90

the ditch, hugging the road like a life raft. Halfway back to town, the tan sedan waited. Ricky dared not look up, but he could feel eyes watching him. The hair prickled on his neck as he passed. Even after he had put a hill between himself and the car, he kept a fast pace.

Overhead the pale, hot sky simmered. Ricky looked up and thought of his mother. He was afraid she would be disappointed.

This time she came to him. "So you couldn't get the airplane, huh?" she asked.

"I'm going to!"

"Why don't you go home?" she said softly. "It's too dangerous trying to fly that plane. Father's waiting for you. He's worried."

"You think I'm going to quit just 'cause of a teeny-weeny flood and a fat old guard?"

"That fat old guard had teeny-weeny bullets that almost killed you," she said, not as softly.

Ricky squinted at the sun. "So you want me to quit?"

"I think you should go home," she said.

Ricky paused before answering. "Okay, I'll go home." When his mother didn't answer, he grinned. "In an airplane!"

Ricky topped the last hill into town and spotted Soledad waiting. Sight of the grubby little girl troubled him. Why had she helped him so much? Who was she? This afternoon, leaving for Rancho Camacho, he'd felt as if he'd abandoned a stray puppy. What was he to do? He couldn't take her along.

Soledad stood and walked out to meet him. "They didn't let you in, did they?" she said, sounding relieved.

Ricky decided not to mention the agent. He shook his head. "I almost drowned."

"*Sí*, the *chubasco* hit here, too." She pointed to where sand had washed across a dip in the road.

"The guard shot at me," Ricky added excitedly.

"I told you they'd shoot," she said.

"You did not! You just said they had big guns."

Soledad frowned. "And what do you think big guns are for?"

Ricky kicked hard at a clump of grass. "I'll sneak in then," he said.

Soledad wrinkled her forehead. "Tell me, what's so important about Rancho Camacho?"

"It's my secret! Don't you have any secrets?"

"*Sí*, I've got lots of secrets. You want to hear them?"

Ricky threw his arms up. "You're *loca*, Soledad."

She giggled. "*Sí*, very *loca*. Very *loca*."

As they walked back toward town, Ricky made plans. If he sneaked into the ranch before sunup, the guards would be tired, maybe asleep. The moon should help him avoid all the prickly pear cactus and thorny mesquite. If not, he'd look like a pincushion before he ever got to the airplane.

The timing needed to be perfect. But what if it wasn't? What if the moon was too bright, or not bright enough? What if somebody caught him? He kicked at the ground in disgust. A person could choke to death on what-ifs!

Ricky paused on the road. "Soledad," he said forcefully. "Why are you following me?"

She shook her head, acting surprised. "You're the one

following me!" she exclaimed, pointing. "I was walking here, and you were walking there. No?"

Ricky pinched his eyes shut with frustration. "I didn't mean right now. I meant this morning, and yesterday. You've followed me everywhere."

Soledad flashed a "who me?" look of innocence, then lowered her head and shrugged. "Maybe you don't like me." She forced her bottom lip out in a pout and started forward again.

"Oh, *caramba*! I like you."

She kept on walking.

"Where are you going?" he called.

Soledad glanced over her shoulder. "I'm going to work."

"To work? Where?"

She smiled mischievously. "Why don't you *follow me* and see?"

Ricky thought a minute. There was nothing else for him to do all afternoon. And he might learn more about Rancho Camacho—Soledad seemed to know more than she let on. "I might hang out with you awhile," he said finally. "But I'm not *following* you."

She smiled and kept walking. Ricky hurried to catch up. What would she get them into next? He had enough troubles already.

Before reaching town, Soledad cut out onto the desert. In a paper grocery bag pulled from her dress, she started collecting leaves from a scrubby bush.

"What are you doing?" Ricky asked.

"These are creosote leaves for the *curandera*. She's a lady who buys them."

"What does she do with them?"

"Sells them to people who are sick." Soledad held up a handful of leaves. "Lots of plants are good for you."

Ricky shook his head doubtfully. He walked over to a tall gray bush—its leaves looked like feathers. He grabbed a thin branch. "What's this one do?"

"No! Not that one—that's the *yerba de flecha*."

"The arrow weed?"

"*Sí*. It makes food leave your body faster than you can eat it."

"It makes you throw up?"

Soledad pointed. "It comes out your tail!"

Ricky let go of the branch and backed quickly away.

When Soledad finished, she tucked the full grocery bag into her sack dress. It made her look like a little Santa Claus. When they returned to the highway, she was unusually quiet. She stomped along, nodding indifferently whenever Ricky spoke. Suddenly she stopped and faced him. "Don't go to Rancho Camacho! Those hombres are *bandidos*. They sell drugs that make people *loco*. They kill people!"

"I know," Ricky said.

"And you still want to go?" She drew away from him with a distrustful look. "I know why you're going to Rancho Camacho!"

"Why?"

"You want to be one of them."

"No!" Ricky blurted. "That's not why." Seeing her doubtful look, he added, "I promise, really."

Soledad did not change her expression. "Follow me!" she demanded angrily.

"Why?"

Soledad started walking.

"I'm not following you!" Ricky shouted.

"Because you're scared!" she yelled, continuing.

Ricky bit his lip. Under his breath he muttered, "I'm not scared of you, you *ratera*."

She kept walking.

Ricky took off running after her. He caught up and, without speaking, followed her into town. A smoldering sun baked the air. Wiping sweat from her forehead, Soledad charged up and down the city blocks, searching. Several times she stopped to gather food from garbage cans.

"Where we going?" Ricky asked impatiently.

Soledad did not answer until she spotted a boy no older than herself. Except for dirty underpants, the *ratero* huddled naked beside a sewer drain. He did not look up. His lips moved mechanically, muttering gibberish. Despite the hot sun, the boy bent forward, squeezing his arms between his knees, shivering.

Soledad approached without speaking. She reached down the front of her dress and pulled out the food she'd collected: an old apple, some broken taco shells, and a dried head of lettuce. Gently she laid them on the sidewalk beside the boy, then spoke bitterly. "This is my cousin Santos. He's my best friend."

The quivering youngster stared vacantly into space.

"Your best friend? What's wrong with him?" Ricky asked. "Why is he shaking?"

"We used to play—lots of games. Last year Santos worked for Rancho Camacho. And they gave him drugs." Her voice flared like a match. "Now look! Look! He'll never again be warm!"

Ricky could not avoid staring at the distant, blank look on the youngster's smudged face—the same stare he'd seen on other *rateros*.

Soledad's voice sounded absolute. "No! Don't go to Rancho Camacho again!" She bent over and gave Santos a gentle kiss on the cheek before leaving.

Ricky did not answer. Nothing would stop him from stealing the plane, especially not some grubby *ratera*. And yet the sight of Santos haunted him. Soledad ignored Ricky, forcing a thick silence between them as they walked.

Next Soledad stopped by a small shop and dropped off her leaves. She came out, proudly holding up a thousand-peso bill. "Pretty good, huh! How do you make money?"

Ricky didn't answer. Cripes, all she'd gotten for her work was about thirty cents.

Soledad headed for the business district of town, shoulders lowered, head butted forward. At phone booths she paused, checking for change that might have been left behind. It appeared she had a regular route. She approached each tourist with her hand out, sad faced like a forlorn puppy. If anyone carried a pop bottle, she galloped up and trailed him until he took the last swallow. Then she jumped into his path, offering to dispose of the container. If he surrendered it, she stuffed it into the neck of her dress. Soon half a dozen bottles clinked about as she walked. At the market she stopped to collect the deposit.

No trash can escaped her. Nor did a fruit stand. She ran up to the woman in charge and said something. Ricky could not hear. The lady smiled and handed her an apple. Soledad stopped to pick up a chunk of glass on the street and used it to crack the apple down the middle. Walking over to Ricky, she handed him half. "I told the lady it was my birthday."

"Thanks," Ricky said, hungrily taking a bite. "Is it your birthday?"

"This year I'm really lucky. I think I have two birthdays."

Ricky shook his head but smiled.

Soledad lifted her dress and pulled the money she'd earned from her dirty gray underpants.

Ricky turned his head away.

"How much have *you* earned?" she asked sarcastically.

"I'm not hungry."

Soledad headed down the street but called back, "That's because I feed you."

For the next hour Ricky watched her as she worked. It seemed like such a waste of time, all this work for a few pesos and some garbage food. Suddenly Soledad halted her scavenging and faced him with an accusing look. "Maybe if you'd help, we'd find more," she said bluntly. She turned and scurried down an alley to check the trash behind a store.

Ricky resented her words. He wasn't a homeless street rat! A *ratero*! He was a pilot, down here to steal an airplane with a special radar. By tomorrow he'd be sleeping in a bed and eating from a refrigerator again. Soledad would drop her teeth if she only imagined. He turned and watched three little boys play marbles on the sidewalk. They were naked except for torn and dingy shorts.

Soledad returned. The top of her baggy dress ballooned full like an overstuffed cushion. If the twine around her waist ever broke, they'd have to call a garbage truck. Her skinny legs looked too small to support the load.

"Wait here," she said, waddling off down the street. Fifteen minutes later she returned, her dress empty. Again she began to beg and scrounge. Several times she shot him accusing glances. This irked Ricky, but he pretended to help search. After an hour, he had yet to find anything edible. Soon it would be dark, and they could stop this foolishness.

"You'd die without me," Soledad said, coming up and handing him an overripe mango.

Ricky thought to turn it down, but his hunger made him think better. He took the fruit, peeled it, and gnawed pulp from the hairy seed. Under his breath he mumbled thanks.

"I know how you can help," she called, already rushing down an alley. She returned carrying two large plastic ice-cream buckets. "Let's wash cars." Not waiting for his okay, she scooped up murky water from the gutter.

"What are you doing?" Ricky asked.

"Watch." She stood, shoulders squared, waiting.

One of the buckets leaked, and Ricky chuckled. If Soledad didn't find a customer soon, she'd have an empty bucket. Luckily a tourist's car pulled along the curb. She ran up to the driver, sloshing water on herself and the sidewalk. Ricky couldn't hear what she said, but soon she turned and motioned for him.

"He'll pay us five hundred pesos to wash the car," she said.

Ricky balked. Five hundred pesos was less than a quarter. Already Soledad had started splashing dirty water over the hood and fenders. She rubbed with her bare hands. "I need more water," she whispered. "Don't let him see where you get it."

Obediently Ricky ran down the street, out of sight of the amused American. He dipped up more murky water from the gutter and returned to Soledad. The water smelled of sewer. She dumped the buckets over the car, then expectantly handed them back to Ricky. While he continued to carry water, Soledad kept rubbing. She jumped to reach parts of the roof. Once Ricky returned to find her laying across the hood, reaching for the center. Finally she slopped a full bucket over the front and another over the back. Smiling proudly, she turned and asked for payment.

The young man laughed as he gave her coins. Looking at the car, Ricky could see why. Hand smudges and smeared dirt left the car looking hideous.

"I'd hate to see your wax job," Ricky whispered.

She jabbed his ribs hard with her elbow, continuing to smile and wave good-bye to her customer.

That afternoon they washed half a dozen cars. When Soledad's hands became puffy and raw, Ricky felt guilty and volunteered to swab several while she shuttled water. Only one owner refused to pay, a dressed-up *turista*.

"Five hundred pesos," Soledad insisted, pushing her outstretched hand at the man's stomach.

"Get out of here. You call that a car wash?" the man growled, pointing.

Soledad kept her hand out.

"I said get, you little pig!" The man grabbed her arm and spun her around.

Soledad pulled free, turned, and stuck out her tongue. Ricky had seen enough. Five hundred pesos was spare change. But Soledad had earned it, and so had he! He ran over and filled a single bucket with the sewer water. Soledad saw him approaching the *turista* from the rear and peppered the man with insults to keep his attention.

Broadside, Ricky doused the man. The *turista* froze as if he'd been shocked. Soledad bounded off, clapping her hands. By the time the man caught his breath and thought to mutter obscenities, Ricky was beside Soledad half a block away.

"He got a good bath. No?" Soledad panted, slowing to a walk. "That should cost him another three hundred pesos. Maybe I'll go ask him." Her eyes twinkled as she glanced back. The man in his new clothes was fuming, stumbling around beside his car as if he were lost.

"Please don't do anything to make him chase us," Ricky pleaded.

"Then why did you throw water at him?"

"He called you a pig."

"Ah, you don't think I'm a pig!" She gave him a smile that made him nervous.

"He shouldn't have called you one."

She grinned. "I think you like me!"

Ricky scuffed at the sidewalk with his sandal. "You're not a pig!"

13

Even after a rusty sunset touched the evening sky, Soledad kept working. She ran up to Ricky, waving a can of shoe polish. "Boy, can I make money now!" she exclaimed, prancing about. Ricky helped her pry open the lid. Only a thin ring of black polish rimmed the edges. Soledad's smile fell. "They didn't leave much," she said accusingly.

"That's why people throw things away, because they're used up," Ricky said.

Soledad poked out her tongue. She examined the small tin more closely and then exclaimed, "It's still good! I'll show you." She turned and ran down the sidewalk, approaching black-shoed *turistas* until she found one who agreed to a shine. "Stand still," she ordered, as if preparing to administer a great professional service.

With her fingernails she dug at the polish, smearing it on the shoe bit by bit. Then she spread it with her palm. To buff the shoe, she grabbed the edge of her sack dress and rubbed, nearly sitting on the man's ankles to make her dress reach. The man glanced about, embarrassed.

Ricky had always figured people lived like Soledad because they were lazy. But never in his life had he seen anyone work this hard. The long day showed in her weary smile. And still she worked. After finishing, she collected her money and motioned Ricky to follow.

"Cripes, Soledad. Aren't we about done?" he called.

"*We* have not worked so hard." She emphasized the *we*.

Soledad didn't seem to know how to walk slowly. Ricky trotted to keep up. The sandals chafed his feet. Finally they reached a section of town where the shops and restaurants remained open after dark. Already, dim streetlights glowed above the bustling street. Soledad walked directly up to the well-dressed shoppers, both Mexican and *turista,* and started begging, her palm extended.

At home Ricky felt guilty whenever he didn't help with work. But here, why should he? He wasn't a *ratero*. But he did, and finally he stood near Soledad and started holding out his hand to shoppers. Smiling, he looked over at Soledad. "Well, how am I doing?"

She scowled. "Beggars aren't happy—don't smile!"

Ricky frowned and kept begging. "Please, señor. Please, señorita. Please, señor," he repeated monotonously. Some people looked past him as if he weren't there. Others brushed him aside with a look of disgust. But several stopped. They dug into their pockets or

purses and found coins. Soledad glanced over and nodded her approval.

"Do you work this hard every day?" Ricky asked.

She shook her head. "Most days I work harder."

Ricky wondered how she spent her meager earnings.
He used his share of the car-washing money to buy two
hot tacos. He offered her one.

"I'll help you earn money, but I won't help you waste
it," she said, scurrying toward another *turista*.

Ricky stood with his mouth full, chewing. He was
tired of begging, scrounging, digging, and grubbing. He
looked forward to getting away from this city. Tomorrow, he promised himself. Tomorrow! He was one plane
ride away from escaping this hellhole.

From the rear, Soledad approached a heavy man in
dark pants and a flowered shirt. He carried a large paper
bag of food from the taco stand. Even in the fading light,
his bald head gleamed as if polished. She ran in front of
the man, hand extended. He brushed her aside.
Doggedly she rushed back and held out her hand. This
time he shoved her and knocked her down. Then the
man turned sideways, and Ricky saw his face. It was one
of the DEA agents who had visited the house, the blimp
Dad called Dexter. Sight of the man jarred Ricky. This
was the second DEA agent he'd seen.

The paunchy, bald agent strutted with self-importance. He crossed the street and crawled into a dark
sedan. Soledad stood slowly, rubbing her head and
squinting hard. Ricky had learned to recognize that look,
and it spelled trouble. She tightened her lips and circled,
keeping out of the glow of the streetlights. Now it was

nearly dark. Seconds later she appeared from the shadows, directly behind the agent's car. Inside, the big man had opened his bag and was eating.

Ricky saw Soledad crouch and glance around. Then she rolled under the rear of the car. After a minute her skinny arm reached out around the front tire. Ricky stifled a laugh. The goofy girl was fumbling with the air valve, letting air out of the tire.

Ricky moved forward. Only thing better than a flat tire was two flat tires. Or maybe three or four. For that Soledad would need help. Ducking low, he angled toward the car. Then silently he dropped to the pavement and squirmed under the rear axle.

Soledad looked back with a start, then smiled and held a finger to her lips. Ricky nodded and reached out around a rear tire. If the agent opened the door, Ricky was ready to roll out the other side and run. He knew Soledad would do the same.

Their task took nearly ten minutes. The sound of people and the loud blaring of street music masked the innocent hiss of air. Each time someone passed on the sidewalk, Ricky and Soledad drew in their arms and waited. Luckily this was not the busy side of the street. Finally the car rested on four flat tires. Underneath there was barely room to move.

Preparing to squirm out, Ricky noticed the rubber gas line coming from the fuel tank to the engine. He motioned for Soledad to wait while he reached up and twisted the stiff tubing. He wedged it tight against the frame. The car wouldn't go far without gas. Quickly Ricky slithered out to the sidewalk.

Dexter sat munching, not noticing that he now rested six inches closer to the ground. Ricky and Soledad crept away from the car to the safety of the alley. They waited, nudging each other with excitement. The agent continued to eat. He scrutinized people as they walked past. Ricky did not mention that he knew the man.

Soledad bounced with impatience. A mischievous and challenging look glimmered in her eyes as she picked up a small rock. Before Ricky could stop her, she pitched it and hit the sedan's rear bumper. From the shadows of the alley, they watched the bulky Dexter squirm out and look around. He spotted one of the flat tires and slapped the hood. Then he noticed a second flat and swore. "Worthless piece of junk!" he shouted. As he walked around the car, he cursed and bellowed louder. Viciously he kicked at the last tire and looked angrily up and down the street. Shoppers stopped on the sidewalk to watch the sideshow.

Ricky and Soledad giggled, holding their breath in the shadows. Dexter headed down the street to a pay phone. Seeing the agent so far from the car gave Ricky an idea. This was getting to be fun. "Wait here," he whispered. Keeping the car between himself and the agent half a block away, he ran up and peeked in the window. The bag of food sat on the seat, much of it still not eaten. A red sport jacket caught his eye. It was big enough to be a blanket. And it looked a lot warmer than Soledad's stinky serape.

Ricky inched open the door and crawled in. The keys were still in the ignition. First he rolled up the driver's window and locked the other three doors. Then, food and jacket in hand, he slipped out and locked the driver's door.

As Ricky rejoined Soledad in the alley, Dexter returned. He walked briskly to the car. When the door refused to open, he jerked hard, squinting in the window toward the ignition. A look of dismay crossed his face. He tried the back door, then strode around, grabbing and testing the others. Again he squinted through the window, then kicked the door. "Why me?" he shouted. He shook with anger, letting out a loud bellow. Finally he stumbled back toward the phone, craning his neck to keep an eye glued on the car.

"I have an idea," Soledad giggled. Without explaining, she dashed from the alley.

"Wait! He's getting mad!" Ricky called in a loud whisper.

She kept going, dodging people and slipping through the shadows. Again she stalked the unsuspecting agent. Her actions worried Ricky. No doubt this was to upstage *his* last prank. The thought struck him: Soledad never waffled things. She barged full tilt into everything she did. He could just imagine her flying a biplane. She would never waffle a loop.

While Ricky waited he went through the jacket he'd taken from the agent. Inside a chest pocket he found a shiny gold badge in a leather holder. The engraved name read Dexter Crumm. Ricky smiled. The name Crumm fit the guy to a T.

Examining the leather holder, Ricky noticed something tucked behind the badge in a small slot. He found a picture and some tightly folded money. In the glow of the streetlight, Ricky counted three one-hundred-dollar bills and a single twenty. Almost as an afterthought, he held the photograph to the light and squinted. A hammer pounded in his chest. He was staring at his own picture.

Ricky recognized the picture from his family photo album. It showed him sitting on top of a stacked mesquite-wood fence, holding Grease Rag, their cat. Grease Rag got her name one day when Dad used her long hair to wipe off his hands at the hangar. Everyone thought it was funny except the cat.

Only Dad could have given the agents this picture. Had he sent them down here? Something else caught Ricky's eye. Under the picture someone had written the words "Sparrow Hawk." What was that all about?

Across the street Dexter Crumm hopped and twisted impatiently in front of the open pay phone as if he had to go to the bathroom. With the receiver glued to his ear, he looked as if he were straining on a leash. His billfold lay open on the phone booth's metal ledge.

Soledad threaded through the shoppers and edged up behind the large man. When he raised an arm to gesture angrily, she reached in and swiped the billfold. As quickly, she vanished into the darkness.

A minute later the agent slammed down the receiver and reached for his billfold. Finding the counter empty, he checked his pockets, then looked frantically around his feet. Again he checked his pockets, then howled like a sick heifer.

Giddy with excitement, Ricky cringed and hunkered deeper into the alley. As he stuffed the badge, money, and picture into his pants pocket, he heard Soledad's voice.

"Our gringo isn't happy," she whispered, appearing out of the shadows.

Ricky spun around. "Soledad, you're *loca*," he said, smiling. "Plumb *loca*!"

She smiled back. "*Sí*, very *loca*."

"Give me five!" Ricky put out his hand.

She looked puzzled.

He reached for her small hand and held it palm up, slapping it lightly. Then he held out his hand. "Give me five." Hesitantly she swatted his hand, grinning timidly. Ricky picked up the jacket and bag of food. Together they retreated down the alley. Safely away from the street, Ricky dropped everything and grabbed Soledad's hands. She did not pull away. They laughed, spinning each other in circles. Their dim shadows danced against the brick walls.

Something glowed inside of Ricky. Since Mom died, he had held his feelings close. It protected him, like a wall. And yet here in a dark alley in Mexico, holding hands with a *ratera,* he danced wildly. The faster he moved, the harder he laughed. A flood of emotion brought tears to his eyes, tears he did not want to spit away.

The air tingled with magic. In the moon-paled alley Ricky could not see Soledad's scarred legs, sack dress, and matted hair. Only her jubilant voice floated into the night, a voice he now admitted enjoying. For two days she had helped him, making sandals, loaning him the serape, getting food, and directing him to Rancho Camacho. There had to be something he could do for her.

Their dancing slowed. Ricky motioned. "Let's get out of here." He breathed hard.

"Where to?" Soledad puffed.

Ricky motioned for her to follow. He threaded away from the main boulevard and into the deserted back streets. For the first time all day, Soledad followed him. Above them the three-quarter moon smiled down. Finally Ricky stopped. "Over here," he said, still huffing.

Soledad followed him under a streetlight. In its bright glow Ricky swept his hand widely and bowed. "If you'll please be seated, my lady. Supper is served."

Eyeing him with curiosity and amusement, she sat on the sidewalk.

Ricky opened the bag with a flair. After spreading out two napkins, he tucked another into his collar like a bib and reached over to tuck one in the neck of Soledad's dress. She giggled and playfully pushed his hand away.

"Okay, you do it," Ricky said. "But supper will not be served, except to proper ladies."

She squirmed with anticipation and stuffed a corner of the napkin into the top of her dress.

Ricky pulled two large burritos from the bag and presented them with exaggerated motion. Next came the chips and salsa. He finished by placing a single can of pop between them. This feast for two was the agent's leftovers. No wonder the man was as big as a moose.

They ate in silence, savoring each bite. Every time Ricky glanced up, Soledad seemed to be watching him, her eyes wide with fascination. She tried awkwardly to imitate him. Seeing this, Ricky swallowed the last of his burrito with a satisfied lift of his chin, then dabbed at his lips delicately with the edge of his bib. She did the same.

"Well, Señorita Soledad, was supper to your liking?"

She wrinkled her cheeks. "*Sí*, Señor Ricardo. I liked it very much. And look!" She reached down the front of her sack dress and pulled out the agent's billfold. Eagerly they looked inside. "*Qué bueno! Qué bueno!*" she squealed, holding up two twenty-dollar bills and a few pesos.

Ricky didn't know what to say. The money was stolen. So was the three hundred and some dollars tucked behind the badge in his own pocket. He dared not show Soledad the badge. She might see his picture and ask questions. For now, anyway, he'd keep quiet about his find.

"Here," she said, handing over one of the bills.

He shook his head. "No, Soledad. I don't want it."

A puzzled look clouded her face. "Ricardo, you're the one who's *loco*. No?" she said. "You talk and act funny. Who are you? How come you don't want money?" She held up the bill. "Everybody wants money. You have gringo feet and soft skin, but you aren't like the gringos."

"How do you know?" Ricky said, his answer more forceful than he had intended. "I mean, have you ever had a gringo friend?"

She shook her head.

Ricky avoided her quizzical gaze. "Any ideas where to sleep tonight?" he asked, anxious to change the subject.

She squirreled her cheeks and wrinkled her forehead in thought. Ricky noticed cute dimples when she flashed a smile. "*Sí,* I know where there's a bed and a ceiling to keep off the rain."

"Where?"

Soledad scrambled to her feet. "Come, I'll show you."

Ricky grabbed the big jacket and followed her. They walked a dozen or more blocks to the edge of Mariposa. "Where are we going?" he asked.

"You'll see." She angled off the street into an open lot strewn with garbage and junk. Carefully she picked her way over to an old rusted and abandoned car. The windows were all broken.

She swept her arm around and bowed, presenting the car like a game-show hostess. "There."

He stared, dumbfounded.

"Do you like it?" Her eyes filled with eager anticipation.

Ricky struggled to find words. He did not want to disappoint her. "Uh, yeah. Sure. Would you like the front or the backseat, Señorita Soledad?" He reached to open a door for her.

She stepped back, shaking her head. "I don't sleep here. I'll be back tomorrow."

"Where will you sleep?"

"That way." She pointed evasively. "I'll get you my serape."

Ricky held up the agent's warm jacket. "This will do."

"Okay. Good night, Ricardo."

"Good night, Soledad."

A fearful look stole over her face, then she turned and ran. The look puzzled Ricky. Why wouldn't she stay here and sleep? He watched her disappear into the night, then turned to examine the junked car. Even in the dark, springs were visible, poking up through the cushions. A strange, rancid smell filled the cab. Carefully, Ricky brushed small chunks of glass off the crusted backseat and crawled in. Anything had to be better than sharp gravel. He pulled the huge jacket around himself and stretched out, squirming until he found a comfortable position.

Again Ricky sensed that he was changing. The sights, the sounds, the people, how they lived, everything: somehow he was drawn to it. He felt a part of it, and it was as if it had always been a part of him. Exhausted from the day's excitement, he dozed off.

Dreams came. Once more his normal dreams did not come to him. Not the ones of being an astronaut or flying the Bell X-1. He dreamed, instead, of his mother. "You have to take better care of yourself, Ricky," she scolded kindly. Then her look grew severe. "You stole money today. Why?"

"But, Mamá," Ricky said, "I didn't really steal it. I found it in this jacket."

"You stole that also," she said.

"I'll give it back," Ricky promised.

She nodded and disappeared.

The dream moved to an old temple, where an Aztec king ruled from a jeweled throne, scepter in hand. At his side waited a queen mounted on a magnificent white stallion, her royal dress glinting with gold and beads. A thin veil covered her face and hid her beauty. From a courtyard a crowd of people stood and whispered about her in hushed, reverent tones. Wind lifted the queen's veil, and Ricky recognized the impish smile and dimpled cheeks. It was Soledad!

"Ricardo," called a faint voice from behind.

Ricky looked around in his dream but saw no one. Then he woke up with a start. A coil spring jabbed his side, and the musty smell of the old car hit him. How long had he slept? Had he heard a voice?

"Ricardo," cried a hesitant, sobbing voice.

"Soledad?" he said, sitting up.

She appeared as a dark shadow in the open doorway.

Ricky still imagined her stunning beauty and proud shoulders from the dream. "What's wrong?" he asked.

Still she sobbed.

Ricky crawled from the car and stood so he could see Soledad's face in a dim wash of light. Her left eye puffed closed and a cut at the corner of her mouth glistened with blood.

"What happened?" Ricky exclaimed.

Soledad hid her face. "He hit me. He said I'm no good."

"Who, Soledad? Who hit you?"

"*Mi papá,*" she sobbed, her breath jerking.

"Your father?" Ricky exclaimed. "I didn't know you had any family. Aren't you a *ratera?*"

"I'm not a rat!" Her eyes showed deep hurt. "You don't think I'm good either!"

"No, Soledad. I . . . uh . . . I meant, I thought you were *una vaga.*"

"I'm not a vagrant. Why do you think these things about me?" She sat trembling.

Ricky watched her. The dim light outlined her stooped body and hunched shoulders. This was not the mischievous Soledad he'd known for two days. Nor was this the stunning lady from his dream.

Her voice cracked. "I think he's right: I'm no good. That's why he hits me." She shivered, her arms wrapped tightly around her sides.

Ricky peeled off the agent's coat and draped it over her shoulders. "Here, maybe you should sit down." He motioned toward the backseat. The huge jacket hung on Soledad like a tent.

She crawled in and flopped face down.

"Are you all right?"

"No!" She pounded the seat. Then she pressed her small fists to her cheeks, muffling her sobs. "No! Papá is right. I'm no good. Sometimes I think I'll die from being no good."

Awkwardly Ricky reached for one of her hands. "Don't say that. Think about when you were happy. It helps me when I'm sad." He didn't tell her how very often that was.

"I'm never happy." Her voice was barely a whisper.

"I was dreaming about you before I woke up," Ricky said. Hearing silence, he continued. "I dreamed you were a queen, sitting on a big white stallion. You were beside an Aztec king. The people all whispered about how pretty you were."

"What people?" she whimpered.

"A whole bunch of people in a big courtyard."

"You have *loco* dreams," she grumped, but looked up.

"I'm not *loco*. I've seen you help your cousin Santos. Look how you've helped me. Lots of people don't do things like that." Ricky pointed at her heart. "That's what makes you pretty."

"What's that?" she pouted. "My belly?"

"No, silly, your heart. That's where your heritage is." Ricky wished he didn't sound so much like his dad.

"What's heritage?"

"It's what's really you. All the good . . . of the Aztecs and Mayans. You know . . . other people, like the Toltecs and the Mixtecs. They're your brothers and sisters even if they lived a long time ago. You come from great people. They were brave, and so are you. I know, 'cause I've watched you."

Soledad's sobs faltered as she listened to his words.

He grew bolder. "Yes," he said. "Montezuma—he's inside of you. He helped you throw that rock at the chef. He helped you give Santos food. Tonight when I saw you on the white stallion beside the throne, you were real pretty. You still are."

"I think you've been drinking tequila like *mi papá*," she muttered.

"Shhhhh, you are pretty. Nobody can take away what's inside of you."

"I rode a great white stallion once," she blurted.

"You did?"

"*Sí*." She rolled over and rubbed her wet cheeks with the back of her fists. "He wasn't white, but I think maybe his left ear was white. . . . *Sí*, his left ear was white."

"Where did you ride a stallion?"

She scratched at her leg. "One night the circus was in Mariposa. I didn't have money, so I went behind the tent and jumped on their donkey."

"A donkey!"

"*Sí*. A real nice donkey with a white ear!" Her voice grew proud. "Like in your dream."

118

Ricky nodded.

"You say nice things," she whispered, yawning. "Say more."

"Many great people are inside of you. They make you a great person, Soledad."

"People are inside of me?" she interrupted with disbelief.

Ricky grinned and pointed to her head. "They're in your memories and in your heart. . . . Lots of them. Remember them, don't ever forget."

Soledad relaxed. "Say more." Her breath softened, growing deep and regular.

Ricky no longer knew what he believed. It was as if he were talking in a daze. As for Soledad, she shouldn't have to live the way she lived. He continued. "Feel them, Soledad, feel them. They were brave and good people. They help you and touch everything you do. They're your heritage. Be proud of them. Be proud of yourself." Ricky paused and tucked the jacket closer around her shoulders.

Soledad had fallen sound asleep.

He looked down at the huddled girl. Deliberately he bent over and placed a gentle kiss on her cheek. Then quietly he crawled over into the front.

Thoughts muddled in his mind. Why had he kissed her? Did he really believe the stuff he'd said? Shivering, he stretched out on the rotted and torn seat. Tomorrow he would go to Rancho Camacho. Early, before first light, he'd sneak in. But first a long and cold night lay ahead. He feared it. Goose bumps covered his bare arms. He changed positions, and a spring poked him.

Ricky did not have to worry about oversleeping. All night he twisted and shivered and tried to bury his bare arms deeper into the rough and torn seat. Before the first sign of daybreak, he sat up. He looked back at Soledad, fast asleep. According to his plan, he should be headed for Rancho Camacho now. But he couldn't leave until he was sure his friend would be okay.

Frustrated, he leaned against the closed door and hugged his knees tight to his chest, waiting. Never before had he been this cold. A thought bumped through his head. How cold had Soledad's cousin Santos been last night? The boy didn't even have a shirt. Did he ever quit shivering? The question haunted Ricky.

Recalling his words to Soledad, Ricky felt embarrassed. Was everything he had said to calm her down just a bunch of blabber? Cripes, he'd carried on worse than Dad. His thoughts of Dad right now were good ones. He would give anything to have him here.

There were so many questions in his mind. What about the dream? About Mom? The airplane? And the guard with the gun? Why did the DEA agent have the picture with "Sparrow Hawk" written on the bottom? The questions confused Ricky, and he ended up gazing out of the broken windows, not thinking at all, just waiting for the first light of day to streak the sky. If he made it home, he'd never complain about the heat again.

The air grew colder even as a red glow melted bright across the horizon. Ricky waited, shivering. Was it possible to get so cold you never warmed up? Again he thought of Santos.

Soledad stirred. Grunting with surprise, she rolled over and looked up. Her bruised eye had swollen closed. Dried blood caked the edge of her mouth. Gingerly she fingered her eye and mouth, wincing. Then her bruised lips parted in a smile. "I bet I don't look like a queen now," she said.

"Morning," Ricky said wearily.

Soledad squirmed upright on the seat. She held out Dexter Crumm's red jacket, an embarrassed look on her face. "You look cold."

"I'm okay," Ricky said.

"*Sí*. And when you die from the cold, I'll tell everybody you're okay." She draped the coat over the seat.

"Thanks," Ricky said, squirming into the coat. He hugged his arms to his body and wallowed in the warmth.

"Why did you help me last night?" Soledad asked.

Ricky shrugged. "What was I supposed to do, chase you away?"

"*Sí*, that's what people usually do."

"You needed help," Ricky said. Then, not considering his words, he continued. "Soledad, you said last night your father beat you?"

She nodded, her eyes big and curious.

"I didn't know you had a family."

"*Sí*, everybody has a family. How can you be born without a *mamá*? You have a *mamá*. No?"

Ricky shook his head. "She's dead." He continued quickly. "What I meant is, I didn't know you had a place to stay."

Once more Soledad looked down uncomfortably. "I

can go home if my *papá* has not been drinking. Last night he drank lots of tequila."

"Why did he hit you?"

"He said I didn't bring home enough food and money."

"For who?"

"I have five brothers and three sisters. Pedro, Enrique, and María are younger than me. I have to bring them food each day, or they don't eat."

"What does your dad do? Doesn't he work?"

"Sometimes . . . to pay for his tequila. Mamá knits, but she's sick." Soledad looked down sadly. "I think she's going to die."

"Mothers should never die," Ricky said stubbornly. "Is she in the hospital?"

"There's no money for that. Only rich people can go to hospitals."

"This is too weird—you mean you got a family and a home but still have to go around and beg?"

"How else can I get food? Does yours fall from the sky?"

Ricky faced Soledad. "I got an idea! Why don't you come with me?"

"Where?"

Ricky jumped out of the car and leaned in her window. He stammered with excitement. "I can't explain everything. But I'm from the United States. If I can steal an airplane from Rancho Camacho, it will stop them from smuggling drugs. Why don't you come home with me . . . if you're not afraid of flying."

122

"You talk *loco*! You're not from the United States; you're like me. You can't fly an airplane."

Now that Ricky had let the cat out of the bag, he nodded excitedly. "Yes, I can! Back home we have a biplane. I've even done a loop." He motioned in a big circle. He didn't tell her he had waffled one alone.

"Do you feel okay? Maybe you got too cold." She crawled from the car with a worried look. "I'll get you food."

"Really, Soledad. I only dressed like this so I could get close to the airplane. That's why I have gringo feet. I can talk Spanish because my father makes me. But I usually talk English." Ricky spewed out several sentences in English. "See!"

"You don't fly airplanes," she insisted, twisting nervously at her dress. "It doesn't matter anyway—I can't go with you. My big brothers and sisters live in Mexico City. They went there to find work. I have to stay and take care of Pedro, Enrique, and María. And who would take care of Mamá? She'll die without me." Soledad's eyes softened with glassy tears. "Maybe she'll die anyway."

"What's wrong with her?"

"She gets real hot and sweats. A man at the market told me the hospital could help Mamá. But that costs too much. Last night I gave her the money from the *turista*. But she says it's not enough." Soledad looked down. "Mamá said I shouldn't steal."

Ricky considered Soledad's words. He knew how it hurt to lose a mother. But what would it be like to watch his mom get more and more sick and not be able to help? That was almost worse! Ricky made up his mind. It wouldn't bring Mom back, but maybe he could help somebody else's mother.

"Soledad, how much money does your mother need?" he asked.

"Lots."

"Would this help?" He pulled out the agent's leather badge holder and withdrew the three hundred-dollar bills and the single twenty.

Soledad's eyes grew big, and she gaped at the money.

"This was in the jacket. I didn't tell you about it because it isn't mine. But I'll work this summer to pay it back."

"Pay it back! To who? You don't even know the man."

"Yes, I do. He's a DEA agent. He's down here trying to find me."

Soledad shook her head in disbelief, still eyeing the money. "You'd do this for me?"

Ricky nodded. "And for your mother."

Grabbing the bills from Ricky's hand, Soledad threw her arms around him, hugging hard and urgently. When she let go she stared once more at the bills. "Keep this." She shoved the twenty-dollar bill back into his hand before he could protest. "I still don't think you're from the United States," she said resolutely.

Ricky pulled out the leather badge holder again. "Look, Soledad." He handed her the picture. "The man that shoved you really was a DEA agent." Ricky showed her the badge. "He had my picture. Why would he have my picture if he wasn't looking for me?"

Soledad stared at the picture and fingered the badge. Doubt filled her eyes.

"Honest, he's looking for me. This isn't how I normally look. That's me." Ricky pointed at the photograph. "See, that's me!"

"Why are the men looking for you?"

"That's a long story. But I can't let him catch me."

Once more she stared in awe at the money in her hand, then back at the picture. "What does this say?" She pointed to the bottom of the picture.

"Sparrow Hawk—that's a small bird. I don't know who wrote that. Or why. But I didn't have the picture with me when I came here. Really."

"I know."

"You do?"

"I looked through your pockets while you were sleeping."

Ricky started to speak, then stopped.

"Maybe you are *loco*. Maybe not," she said. "Last night you said lots of nice things! You don't talk like us."

"Listen, Soledad. Somehow I have to get to the airplane. I had planned on sneaking in this morning before daylight. But I wanted to know if you were all right."

She nodded. "I'm okay. But you can't go to Rancho Camacho. They won't let you in. Here." She handed the picture back, a troubled look on her face.

"No, you keep it. But don't show anyone, okay?"

She glanced warmly at the picture, then stuffed it into her dress.

"Don't show anyone, okay?"

She nodded.

The sun gleamed across the adobe town. Ricky squinted and tugged idly on the door handle. "Maybe I can sneak into Rancho Camacho during the day?"

"No one can sneak in," she said firmly. "You have to go through the gate."

"I tried that," Ricky said. "And they shot at me!"

Soledad toyed with the money and fingered the twine wrapped around her waist. "They don't shoot the taco runner."

16

"Taco runner?" Ricky studied Soledad. "Who's the taco runner?"

"Hernando."

"Who's Hernando?"

Soledad avoided Ricky's stare. "He's one of the muchachos who beat you up. He takes food to the *bandidos* with his bicycle."

"You mean you saw me get beaten up?"

"*Sí.*"

"Why didn't you help me?"

Soledad giggled. "Did you hear the police car come to chase the muchachos away?"

Vaguely he did remember the siren. He nodded. "Kinda. But I never saw any police."

She grinned, then puckered her cheeks and let go a curdling and familiar siren call. Finishing, she puffed out

127

her chest. "Pretty good. No? The muchachos ran real fast."

Ricky burst out laughing. "That was you?"

She bounced excitedly. "*Sí, sí*. They ran, *muy rápido*."

"Those jerks stole everything I had. Are they your friends?"

"I have many amigos."

"Which one is Hernando?"

"The one who can't walk—you bit his toe."

"Yeah, after he kneeled on my face! No way will he let me be taco runner; I bit him real hard."

"He'll let *me* use the bicycle," Soledad said, expanding her chest again. "And I'll let *you* use it. Hernando won't know."

"Why would he lend you his bicycle?"

"Because Hernando can't ride with a hurt foot. If he doesn't bring food, the hombres will get real mad. When Hernando is sick, sometimes he lets me ride—the hombres pay me." She held up four fingers. "I've been the taco runner four times."

"But I won't be bringing the bicycle back."

Soledad thought a moment, then shrugged. "He shouldn't go to Rancho Camacho anyway. Someday they'll give him drugs the way they did my cousin Santos. Maybe without a bicycle Hernando won't go to the ranch anymore. That would be good."

"What if he gets mad at you for losing his bicycle?"

"Lots of people get mad at me. He won't hurt me." She smiled mischievously. "Because I'm a girl."

Ricky studied her. She acted bulletproof. But her sobs from the night before hung in his mind.

"Stay here," she said. "I'll try to get the bicycle." She turned and ran.

"Wait! I'm not sure I want to be the taco runner!"

She kept running, weaving among the abandoned junk. Soon she bobbed out of sight.

Ricky held his head and groaned. Couldn't she stop and think for just a second? Taco runner? Was this another of her half-baked ideas?

As the sun rose, the morning air warmed quickly. Ricky yawned and crawled back into the car to wait. He stretched out. With his foot he bumped the mirror, deflecting the sun's glare. Riding a bicycle in through the front gate seemed risky. He hadn't forgotten the sting of gravel kicked up by the guard's machine gun. And yet what other choice did he have? Yawning, he waited. Lack of sleep tugged at his eyelids, and the warm jacket helped him doze off.

The sound of metal rattling and clanking jerked Ricky awake. He heard the crunch of tires on gravel and sat upright.

"You're now the taco runner!" Soledad exclaimed, skidding to a stop. "Here's Hernando's bike."

Ricky stepped stiffly from the car.

With pride, Soledad displayed an old, fat-tired, single-speed bicycle. The rusty frame showed only patches of the original green. Twine held a twisted metal basket to the bent handlebars. "It's a good bicycle. No?"

Ricky shook his head. "Will it make it to the ranch?"

She nodded. "*Sí! Sí!* Hernando said to ride to Rancho Camacho at eleven o'clock. You must go to the men in the big building. They'll give you money and tell you what food to buy."

"The big building—that's where the Skyhawk is."

Soledad looked puzzled. "Skyhawk?"

"Yeah, the airplane I'm going to fly away from the ranch."

She wrinkled her forehead. "I still don't think you can fly an airplane, Ricardo. You're small, and airplanes are real big. They go really high." She spread her arms and tilted them, making a roaring sound.

Ricky laughed. Soledad would love going up in the Baby Great Lakes. She'd pop an artery seeing him do a loop. "I can fly," he said. "When I leave Rancho Camacho, I'll fly over and dip my wings twice, then you'll know it's me." He put out his hand and tilted it side to side.

"Four times," she said.

"Okay, four times."

"Hernando said he always tells the guard he's the taco runner. That's what you should do. He said not to make the hombres mad."

"I guarantee they'll be mad when I get done." Ricky ignored Soledad's worried look. "Hey, are you hungry?"

She nodded.

"Okay, let's eat!" Ricky said. "This morning I choose. Hop up." He swung his leg over the bicycle seat and motioned to the crossbar.

"Where are we going?"

"I'll show you."

She giggled and jumped on. Wobbling, they headed out. Ricky ignored her repeated questions as they bounced over the curb onto the street. "First, take me to your cousin Santos," he said.

"Why?"

"I have something for him."

Soledad gave Ricky a puzzled look but directed him through the back streets. They found Santos huddled in a shaded alley, a piece of cardboard bent around his shoulders. Still he shivered.

"What do you have for him?" Soledad asked.

"Hold the bicycle." Hesitantly Ricky took off the agent's red jacket and laid it in front of Santos. "This is for you," he stammered.

Santos kept shivering and stared right past Ricky with his dark, hooded eyes.

Soledad dropped the bicycle on its side. "You have to help him."

Together they wrestled the jacket onto the rubbery-limbed boy. It was large enough to hang over his knees. Ricky zipped it up as far as he could. "I hope this keeps him warm," he said.

Soledad smiled. "*Sí*. Santos would say *gracias* if he could."

Back on the bicycle, Soledad teetered eagerly on the crossbar in front of Ricky. "Where are we going to eat?" she pleaded.

"The Restaurante del Sol."

She looked back and smiled. "Good! The chef will chase us with his knife."

"He won't chase us this morning," Ricky said. It was important to him that they go back to the same restaurant. He wanted Soledad to know that all of life wasn't digging through garbage cans and being chased with butcher knives.

She nodded insistently. "*Sí,* he's always there. I'll throw big, big rocks."

Ricky kept pedaling. Houses and streets slipped past. Gradually Soledad leaned back against Ricky's chest. Her shoulder pressed gently against his. Looking down, he saw her eyes close. A soft smile creased her lips.

Ricky avoided sharp turns and bumps. When he slowed in front of the restaurant, Soledad opened her eyes and sat forward. She grinned. "I can't wait for him to chase us."

Ricky parked the bike directly in front of the entrance. Getting off, he motioned to the big glass front door with a sweep of his hand. "We will be eating inside today, my lady."

17

"Stop making jokes," Soledad said.

Ricky stepped toward the restaurant door. "C'mon."

Worry clouded her face. "No, we can't eat inside, you dummy. They won't let us." She backed away from the door. Ricky tugged on her arm, but she struggled loose. "No! We can't go inside."

Ricky turned. "I'll go ask. Wait here."

"No, no, no!" she stammered, grabbing at his arm.

Ricky dodged her hand. "I'll be right back." He slipped through the front door.

At midmorning the restaurant was not busy. Three men, hired by the restaurant, walked table to table singing songs. One played a guitar. At the cash register the host glanced up and saw Ricky. He pointed sternly back out the door.

Ricky walked forward, holding up the twenty-dollar bill Soledad had insisted he keep. He spoke quickly.

133

"Today is a special day, and I want to buy my friend a good meal." He pointed out to where Soledad waited beside the bike. She shifted from foot to foot, peering in through the window. "We won't be any trouble, I promise," Ricky said. "And I'll pay you before we eat if you want." He guessed that the man would like American money. Mexicans usually did.

The man breathed deeply and looked down at the bill, then out at Soledad.

"Please," Ricky said. "I'll even leave a tip."

A thin but understanding smile broke over the man's face. He nodded as he reached out and took the bill. "Okay, you can sit over there." He pointed to a booth in the back corner, away from other customers. "But if you cause trouble, you'll have to leave."

"*Gracias, gracias,*" Ricky blurted. He ran out the door and motioned. "He says we can eat, Soledad. Come, quick!"

Her eyes darted back and forth like a scared deer's. "It will cost *mucho*!"

It struck Ricky—this was the first normal thing he had done with her. Why did it seem so awkward and scary? "I have the twenty dollars you gave back to me," he said.

Still she eyed him with doubt.

"C'mon. Do I have to carry you?"

She turned and ran toward the edge of the building.

"Where are you going?"

Soledad stopped beside a murky puddle. She reached down and splashed muddy water on her hands and face.

134

Using her dress, she wiped roughly at her matted hair. "I should look good," she said, returning hesitantly.

Inside the door, she eyed the kitchen, her body tense and ready to run. "This way, please," said the waiter, as if escorting regular patrons. Still singing, the three musicians turned curiously to watch. Several customers looked up from their meals. Ricky walked boldly toward the far table. Soledad stole along behind, as if being led to her execution. When she squirmed into the booth, she slid nearly under the table to hide herself from the kitchen.

"Here," said the waiter, handing them menus. "I'll be back to take your order."

Soledad waited until the man crossed the room, then slid back up and said with a hushed voice, "You're dumb! We shouldn't be here. *Qué estúpido! Qué tonto! Qué loco!* If the chef sees us, he'll kill us." She leaned over and glanced toward the kitchen, then out the front window.

"I hope he doesn't kill us until we finish eating," Ricky said, trying to keep from smiling. "I hate dying on an empty stomach."

Soledad poked out her tongue. "And maybe you'll have no stomach after he catches you." She picked up her glass of water and downed it.

"What are you having, señorita?" Ricky asked casually, looking over his menu.

For the first time Soledad opened her menu and stared at the long list of foods. "They have all these things?" she exclaimed. "No wonder they have so much garbage."

She kept looking.

"I can only read the prices," she announced. "And I think they want too much."

"This isn't costing you a single peso. You can have anything you want. I'll read it to you." Slowly he read down the menu.

"Too much, too much, too much," she repeated after each item until Ricky finished.

"Have you decided?" asked the waiter, returning to the table.

Ricky nodded. "I'll have the large *huevos rancheros* with extra salsa," he said. "And a large glass of milk."

Soledad searched frantically up and down the menu.

"And you, señorita?" The waiter turned to Soledad.

"This," she blurted, pointing to the cheapest thing she could find.

"An order of toast?" asked the waiter.

"No way, señorita," Ricky said. "Bring her the same thing I ordered."

Soledad shook her head, but the waiter wrote down the new order. He winked at Ricky, then walked away.

"They'll want thousands and thousands of pesos," Soledad hissed. "When we finish, we better run real fast."

"I've already paid him. Nobody is going to chase us anywhere."

"The cook won't care—he'll still kill us! Why don't you save the money? It's easier to run."

"Soledad," Ricky said. "This is just my way of saying thank you for all your help."

She glanced down, avoiding his eyes. When she looked

up, she tilted her head quizzically. "You thank people by wasting money and getting them killed?"

Ricky grinned. "I suppose we can tell the waiter to forget the whole thing. I'll get my money back, and we can go look for some garbage cans."

Worry flickered in her eyes.

"Just kidding," he said.

Slowly she relaxed. When the waiter brought the plates filled with eggs and salsa and potatoes, Soledad stared. Ricky wondered if she had ever eaten a nice meal prepared for her. She reached to grab some food.

"Use these," he said, holding up his fork and knife.

Awkwardly she lifted her fork and knife, attempting to imitate Ricky's deft movements. She tried to pile half the meal on each forkful. Several times the load spilled back to the plate. "This doesn't work," she said, gripping her fork like a baseball bat.

"Take little bites."

"If I do that, I'll die before I get full."

Silently they ate. Once Ricky looked up and found Soledad shoveling food into her mouth with her scooped hand. Their eyes met. With an impish smile, she wiped her hand on her dress and picked the fork up once again.

Concluding a song at another table, the three musicians approached Ricky and Soledad. Soledad moved quickly to escape the booth but didn't have time. Trapped, she slid back against the wall, cowering. The men smiled and started singing in harmony. Soledad's eyes raced back and forth between Ricky and the men. Ricky tried to smile and act casual. When the singers finished, they nodded and bowed politely and went on to another table.

"They sang just for us!" Soledad exclaimed.

Ricky smiled. "Just for us."

"Would you like anything else?" asked the waiter, stopping by their table.

Soledad shook her head vigorously.

"Yes, ice cream for both of us," Ricky said.

The waiter nodded and left.

"Ice cream?" Soledad said, excitement in her eyes.

Ricky grinned. "If they kill us, we might as well have ice cream in our bellies!"

She stuck out her tongue, then chuckled. "He doesn't even know we're here."

"Who, the waiter?" Ricky asked.

"No, the chef."

"Let's keep it that way."

Still she laughed. "I think maybe sometime I'll tell him. I'll tell him I sat right here and ate his food, and he didn't know." She giggled.

"Here you are." The waiter served their dessert.

Ricky watched Soledad eat her ice cream. She ballooned each mouthful back and forth in her cheeks before swallowing. Her looks toward the kitchen became more frequent and more defiant. Sitting in the lion's den, eating his food, had left her squirming with excitement.

"The chef has one knife as big as a broom!" she whispered.

The waiter stopped by the table with the change from Ricky's twenty-dollar bill. "Thank you very much," he said with a slight bow and a hint of humor.

Soledad looked up, ice cream smeared around her mouth. "You're welcome *very much*."

Standing to leave, Ricky placed a thousand-peso coin on the table for a tip.

"What are you doing?" Soledad whispered.

"It's a tip—to say thank you."

"But you gave him a thousand pesos?"

Ricky nodded. "That's only thirty-five cents. I should be leaving a dollar."

She grabbed for the coin. "It's better to say thank you to me."

Ricky stopped her arm and motioned her out the door. Once more she reached swiftly for the coin. Ricky swatted her hand. "No! Now, come on, let's go."

"You're *loco*," she muttered, walking reluctantly from the table. "Some days I work all day and don't earn a thousand pesos."

Out front Soledad paused to look back through the window. "He doesn't even know we were here."

"Let's go," Ricky said, grabbing the bike and turning it around.

"He should know," she said stubbornly. "I think I'll tell him." Suddenly she bolted for the front door and ran inside.

"Cripes, Soledad, don't do it!" It was too late. Ricky pressed his face against the window. Soledad had crossed the dining room to where a swinging door opened into the kitchen area. She pushed open the door and put her thumb and index finger in her mouth. Ricky heard a sharp whistle. "You fix good food!" she yelled.

Soledad bounded out the front door, her legs and arms churning. "Now—pedal fast!" she cried. "Go! Go fast!"

Ricky stood poised, leg over the seat. He braced the bicycle as she vaulted onto the crossbar, nearly knocking him over.

"Hurry! Hurry!" she stammered.

Ricky pushed off and strained to get the overloaded rusty bike up to speed. Soledad kicked her feet at the air and shook the handlebars to assist. "Sit still!" Ricky grunted, looking back.

The chef lumbered out the front door, his big stomach swaying. He lunged into pursuit.

Again Soledad took to kicking and bouncing on the crossbar. The bike wobbled and weaved down the street. Ricky struggled to keep it upright. "Sit still!" he ordered.

Soledad looked back and quit wiggling. "He doesn't

have his knife." Her voice cracked with disappointment. "And he isn't chasing us very fast."

Ricky glanced over his shoulder. The big chef had slowed to a stumbling trot. His shouts echoed. Ricky relaxed. "Do you want to go back and lend him a knife?" he asked Soledad.

She jabbed him with her elbow, causing him to swerve. Then she rode silently as if pouting over the chef's halfhearted cooperation. Not until they had crossed town did she speak. She spoke quietly. "It's time now for you to go to Rancho Camacho."

Ricky only nodded. He knew it was time, and he felt guilty. What would happen to Soledad?

"The *bandidos* will give you money and tell you what food to buy," Soledad said. "You must do what they say."

Ricky had no intention of doing as they said. He'd pretend to be the taco runner only until he made it past the guard. Today the drug smugglers could starve. They would probably lose their appetite anyway after he escaped with the Skyhawk and the radar.

"Where should I leave you?" he asked.

"I'll wait for you near town." Soledad's voice sounded sad and remote.

"I won't be coming back, Soledad."

"*Sí*, I think maybe they'll kill you. It's a mistake for you to be the taco runner."

"I have to do it," Ricky said resolutely. Again they rode in silence. On the edge of town Ricky stopped and let Soledad jump off. "The last time when I walked to

141

Rancho Camacho," he said, "another DEA agent was parked beside the road. I hope he isn't there today."

Soledad squinted out toward the desert. "I don't think it's a very good day to park beside the road."

When she did not continue, he faced her. "Thanks for all the help." He tried to sound casual.

"I'll wait here."

Ricky fidgeted with the handlebars. "Soledad, I said I'm not coming back."

"And I said I'll wait here." She stood resolutely.

"Why don't you come with me?"

"I told you. Who would take care of my brothers and my sister? And Mamá—I have to help her."

Ricky nodded reluctantly. The dusty air was making his eyes water. It wasn't fair that Soledad had to take care of her family. Why should she be the responsible one? Couldn't her dad do something?

"Hurry, get going!" Soledad said.

Not thinking, Ricky turned and hugged her. "I'll come back and visit you, I promise," he said, blinking.

Soledad hugged him back. Her tight clutch felt desperate. Then she let go. She dropped down and sat crosslegged in the dirt. Without looking up she said, "Go— the *bandidos* are hungry. Don't make them mad."

Ricky mounted the bike and headed for Rancho Camacho. A big lump stuck in his throat. He tried not to look back. But topping the first hill, he did. Soledad sat beside the road like a small statue. "Go home," Ricky whispered. "That's where I'm headed."

Soon the hill blocked her from sight. Ricky tried not to think of Soledad. Now he must think of what lay ahead. Fear of the big guard came back to him. In his mind the machine gun thundered loud, and he could almost feel the gravel sting his legs. What if the guard recognized him?

Ricky's legs trembled and grew weak. It felt as if he were riding uphill even when he wasn't. A slight breeze brushed him from the left. He tried to make note of its direction. This would be important for taking off. Was it possible Mom was watching over him? "Mamá, are you there?" he said aloud.

At first she did not come to his mind.

"I'm really scared," he said. "What if I can't get the airplane started? What if the guard shoots me?" Ricky paused. "Mamá, I feel wrong leaving Soledad all alone."

"Then why not forget about the airplane?" he heard her say.

Ricky shook his head vigorously. "I'm not a quitter. I couldn't help Soledad anyway. I'm going after the airplane."

"Don't do it for me," she whispered with the breeze.

"But they killed you! Don't you see?"

She did not answer.

"Mamá, don't you see?"

Still silence.

Ricky swallowed and kept riding. "I'm not a quitter," he mumbled. Ahead a different sedan sat parked beside the road. It looked like the one that he and Soledad had worked over the night before. Sure enough, the same bald agent slouched in the seat. Ricky smiled—he still had the guy's badge.

Ricky rode past, afraid to glance over. Again he heard

a camera click. He kept riding. It no longer mattered what pictures anybody wanted to take; he'd soon be inside Rancho Camacho. The agent wouldn't follow him there. Ricky resisted the urge to turn and stick out his tongue. Or to throw the badge in through the car window. Soledad would have done it in a blink. Ricky kept pedaling. The car did not follow.

In minutes Ricky steered the bike down the rutted clay road toward the ranch. His shoulders cramped from gripping the handlebars too tightly. The urge to turn back grew stronger. If his mom didn't care about the plane, maybe it wasn't that important.

He heard voices in his head. Voices that taunted, "You're a quitter. Go back home where you belong. You can't steal that airplane!" "I can too!" Ricky muttered under his breath. He pedaled deliberately around the last bend.

A different man was on guard. This one, a tawny Mexican, leaned against the gate. His pockmarked face and cold stare sent a shiver through Ricky. *"Dónde está Hernando?"* the man called, mechanically holding up his hand.

"He hurt his foot," Ricky answered in Spanish. "Today I'm the taco runner." He pulled to a stop.

The man eyed him with suspicion. "Maybe you're lying to me."

Ricky fought the urge to turn and pedal wildly away from the guard and his machine gun. He forced a smile. "Don't you want tacos today?"

The man regarded him, then swung his machine gun

around and pushed open the gate with the barrel. "The tacos aren't for me." He motioned Ricky past.

Too scared to breathe, Ricky nodded and pedaled forward. Any moment he expected bullets to rip into his back. His chest started pounding for air. He gulped hard and rode fast down the long hill toward the compound. Sweat dripped from his forehead and stung his eyes.

Beside the main compound a huge white hacienda sprawled, surrounded by green lawn. The lawn looked out of place on the dry desert. Red tiles blanketed the hacienda's roof. Bright pink trim outlined the doors and windows. On the porch several men huddled intently. Closer to the big equipment shed and the runway sat a series of jacales, small mud-wattle houses made of cottonwood logs supporting mud and bear-grass roofs. Salted meat hung in strips from many of the rafter ends. Beside these hung long strings of red chili peppers. Short stacks of mesquite wood guarded the entrances.

Two laughing Mexican cowboys were prancing their horses around a clearing. The vaqueros sat tall in their *charro* saddles with saddle horns as big and round as coffee cans. Taking turns, they swung their reatas, snaking the long horsehair lariats at a post fifty feet away. Ricky had heard how these vaqueros roped stray cattle to milk them. Maybe the people of Rancho Camacho weren't drug smugglers.

But then why would they have so many airplanes? And why the rolled barbed-wire fences and the guards?

The vaqueros paid Ricky scant notice as he pedaled toward the equipment shed. Several pigs and goats wandered about. Ricky had to swerve to miss one old sow that grunted across in front of the bicycle.

Approaching from this direction, Ricky could not see the Skyhawk. What if it was gone? He circled the building. Then he saw it, and his heart began skipping beats! The plane was backed just inside the big open panel doors. He drew in a deep, slow breath, trying to calm himself. Quietly he whispered, "Okay, grab your socks. It's show time."

Ricky dropped the bicycle in the dirt and peeked through the side door. Beyond the Skyhawk a guard lounged against a large stack of hay bales. Except it didn't look like hay. The burly man wore bibbed coveralls like a farmer's. A machine gun lay balanced across his knees.

Ricky eased inside the door. Two men near the back worked shoveling the green leafy material from opened bales into several long rows of trash compactors. Marijuana, Ricky guessed. Bags of the compressed plant were stacked six or seven high against the shed walls.

The men traded idle comments. "*Ayúdame, Juan!*" a worker shouted. The other worker walked over to help lift bags to a top row. In front of the Skyhawk a fourth man moved into view, patrolling with a machine gun slung carelessly from his shoulder. He reached the far side of the big sliding door, turned, and paced back.

Ricky ducked behind a barrel. Crouching, he watched

the guards and the workers. The big doors were open; that was good. They were probably opened for light and to keep the building cooler. The layout, however, bothered Ricky.

The Skyhawk could be taxied straight forward, but the guards would shoot him to ribbons before he got the engine going. And even if the plane could be started, it would be a sitting duck until it gained speed out onto the runway for takeoff. No one could steal the plane with it guarded this way.

Ricky remained crouched behind the barrel. An angry frustration welled up in his gut—the same feeling he got when he had been beaten up by the bullies at school. He could hear them standing over him and taunting, "Get up and fight, you quitter!" But each time he did they knocked him back down.

Here beside the hangar he felt as if he'd been knocked back down and couldn't get up. His whole life had been knocked down and would *never* get up! The airplane sat only feet away, but it might as well have been on a different planet—trying to steal it would be suicide. Carefully Ricky backed out the door.

"*Alto!*" shouted the guard.

Ricky glanced up.

The guard with the coveralls held his machine gun pointed across the shed at Ricky. "*Alto!*" he shouted again.

For a split second Ricky thought to run. But outside he would have to cover too much open ground. Swallowing to keep his heart from beating up out of his throat, he stopped.

"Quién eres?" the guard demanded, motioning him closer.

"I'm the taco runner," Ricky stammered in Spanish, trying to keep his voice steady as he moved forward.

"Dónde está Hernando?"

"He hurt his foot yesterday. He . . . uh . . . told me to ride his bicycle. Said I should get food for you."

The workers stopped and stared. The outside guard also walked over. All four scrutinized him with hard stares.

"Why were you leaving?" growled the guard in Spanish. He fingered his suspenders and flared his nostrils when he spoke.

"I was leaving 'cause I didn't think this was the right place."

"The right place for what?" the guard said, glaring.

"Where you wanted food."

"How can you tell if I am hungry? Ah, all you taco runners will go to hell someday, and maybe I'll help send you there." He raised the machine gun and aimed.

"No!" Ricky screamed, and dived for the floor, directly under the right wing of the Skyhawk.

All four men hacked with laughter. The guard lowered his weapon. "Come!" he snarled.

Ricky stood to his feet, cowering.

The gruff man stepped forward and grabbed Ricky by the neck. His fingers dug deep. "You tell Hernando to be here tomorrow." The guard poked the gun barrel into Ricky's cheek.

"I will! I will!"

The man let go and held out a hundred-thousand peso

bill. "Go to the Restaurante San Miguel. Get six burritos and eight tacos. Ride *rápido*! If the food is cold, I'll twist your ears off and feed them to the buzzards. If you steal the money, I'll find you and kill you!"

Ricky nodded, putting the money into his pocket.

"Don't forget salsa," he added.

"*Sí, mucha salsa*," the workers murmured.

"*Ándale!*" barked the guard, shoving Ricky hard with the gun barrel.

Ricky ran frantically across the shed and out the side door. Coughing laughter split the air. Jumping onto the bike, Ricky pedaled hard through the compound and up the long road to the front gate. The guard swung open the gate and watched with an icy glare. Ricky stared straight ahead and kept pumping at the pedals. His chest burned.

Not until he reached the main road did he dare stop. Heart pounding, chest heaving, he bent over the handlebars and gulped air. The world spun and tilted. Ricky braced his feet until bit by bit his heart slowed. Everything steadied. He was alive, but failure numbed his thoughts and made him wish he weren't. He pedaled slowly toward town. Nothing ever worked out. Maybe it was because he was dumb! Maybe he *was* a quitter! Tears swelled into his eyes. Over and over he spit at the ditch. Still everything blurred.

Consciously Ricky avoided thoughts of his mother and dad. As for Soledad, this would only prove to her that he couldn't fly an airplane. She would always think him a liar. It wasn't fair, Ricky thought. Nothing was fair.

The air felt heavy. His tires felt flat. What could he

do? Where could he go? It would be difficult now to get home. If only he hadn't chopped off his hair and thrown away the ID card—what a stupid move! One thing was for sure, he'd never go back to Rancho Camacho. Twice he'd been lucky not to be shot.

Ricky rode slowly toward town. He scarcely looked at cars that passed. He did notice that the drug agent's car was gone, but that meant nothing now. Near where it had been parked, he swerved to avoid a basketball-sized wasp nest lying on the highway. Wasps still crawled and swarmed about.

This whole harebrained idea had been stupid. Who was he kidding? He *was* a quitter. Over and over he let the words soak into his brain, into his heart, and into his soul. He was a quitter! And he didn't care. He was beaten.

Nearing Mariposa, Ricky slowed, then stopped. He couldn't face Soledad. There was no way to prove to her he hadn't lied. That was why she had been so sure he would be back. Whatever happened, he didn't want to be seen riding Hernando's bicycle. He jumped off the two-wheeled piece of junk and gave it a hard angry shove into the ditch. It stayed upright for ten or fifteen feet, then wobbled and crashed with a clank as the basket hit the dirt.

The easiest thing to do would be to enter Mariposa from a different direction. It really didn't matter where, as long as he avoided Soledad. Slowly he picked his way out between the clumps of bear grass and cactus into the desert. Maybe the buzzards would get him. They probably didn't eat quitters!

A noon sun burned high in the sky. Hot air rose in shimmering waves on the horizon. Not watching his path, Ricky nearly ran into a tall bush. At first he turned to avoid it. Then he glanced at the long gray branches. He recognized the featherlike leaves of the arrow weed. Soledad had called it *yerba de flecha*. He remembered also everything she had said about the plant.

He turned and walked closer. A crazy idea flickered in his head—a stupid one that could get him into real trouble. Shoot, it could get him killed. He tried to ignore it, but it gained a toehold. Slowly it gripped his thoughts. In that moment all his frustrations and despair evaporated. If the drug runners wanted to pick on a *ratero*, let them try. Nearly tripping, he ran back toward the bicycle.

20

Ricky picked up Hernando's bike, hoping his angry shove hadn't broken anything. He jumped on and headed for Mariposa. No longer did the tires feel flat. If the men wanted food, he'd give them food they would never forget.

Topping the last rise in the road, he searched for Soledad. The familiar squatty shape was gone from beside the highway. As he rode he looked for her. Not that he really cared, of course. It would have just been fun to explain why he was back. She'd twist a gut laughing.

Ricky still had the drug smuggler's money, but he had no idea where to find the Restaurante San Miguel—this was not where he and Soledad had eaten. Nor could he remember the food order given to him. A guard had been squeezing his throat and holding a gun to his head, not exactly ideal conditions for listening.

Several times Ricky stopped and asked directions. The

final turn took him up a short side street. The Restaurante San Miguel was little more than a small café.

When Ricky entered the restaurant, the proprietor looked up. His head tilted back so he could look through glasses slipped low on his nose. He spoke like a stuck record. "Go on, go on, go on," he sputtered, motioning Ricky away. The man's pencil-thin mustache wiggled like a caterpillar when he spoke.

Ricky felt new courage, maybe because he had nothing more to lose. Or was it because he felt like a special person and no one had the right to treat him this way? "I'm here to get food for Rancho Camacho," he said loudly. "Should I ride back and tell them you said no?"

The man's eyes bulged behind his thick glasses. He looked fearfully around to see who might have heard. "N-n-no, don't do that," he stammered in a loud whisper. "I was expecting Hernando."

"Yeah, well, Hernando isn't feeling good."

"Okay, okay. What food do you want?"

Ricky tried to remember what had been ordered. There had been burritos and tacos. But how many of each?

"Well, what do you want?" repeated the man.

"Uh, I think I want five burritos and eight tacos."

"You think!" The waiter looked at him with curiosity and concern.

Ricky nodded, formulating his plan. "Oh, they wanted extra salsa. Lots and lots of salsa."

"For your happiness and good health, I hope you're right." The man shuffled back to the small kitchen. Shortly he shuffled back, carrying the order in a brown paper bag. "That is forty-six thousand, five hundred pesos."

Ricky paid the man. *"Gracias,"* he said, stuffing the change safely in his pocket.

"In that bag are five burritos and eight tacos," repeated the man carefully. "And *mucha, mucha* salsa! I pray to the Virgen de Guadalupe, to Santa Rosalía, and to Santa Rita that you have remembered well."

Ricky hoped so, too, as he pedaled hard toward the highway. The bag of food slid about in the rattling basket. He searched for Soledad as he slowed to catch his breath. Where was she? Again he thought of his plan. Maybe it was just as well Soledad didn't know.

A mile from town he spotted the arrow weed. Riding through the ditch and out onto the desert, he stopped, grabbed the meal bag, and dropped the bicycle near the plant. It was too frightful to think what would happen if this plan didn't work. Quickly he knelt.

Ricky wished he'd asked Soledad what part of the plant was the most potent. With a sharp edge of a rock, he dug down to the roots. One by one he opened the wrapped tacos and burritos. He wiped the roots against his pants and grated white pulp in among the lettuce and sauce. On each he tried to squeeze some juice. It was doubtful the men would notice anything—battery acid probably wouldn't change the taste of Mexican salsa much. It was hot enough to take paint off a barn.

Finishing, he ran to the bicycle and headed toward Rancho Camacho. No longer did the same raw fear weaken his muscles and take away his breath. No longer did failure numb his thoughts. Instead a cautious anger possessed him. It helped to think of Soledad's cousin Santos and what the drug men had done to him. How many other street children had that happened to? Dad had been right: the children weren't *rateros*!

Again Ricky spotted the wasp nest. Several cars had flattened it. Only a few wasps still buzzed nearby. Ricky rode a wide berth around them. The agent had left. Where had he gone?

After leaving the main highway, Ricky pedaled rapidly. Soon there would be no turning back. For a moment, approaching the guard, his heart pounded faster. The guard did not speak. He swung open the gate with a dull, monotonous stare.

"*Gracias,*" Ricky hollered, smiling.

The guard scowled.

Ricky headed down the long hill into the compound. He focused intently on the large equipment shed. How could a huge drug operation like this be run right under the nose of the Mexican police? It seemed like everyone in Mariposa knew about it.

As he pedaled the last hundred yards, Ricky drew in a deep breath. A one-ton truck sat parked near the side door of the big storage shed. He rode along the far side to keep the bicycle hidden. Making sure nobody was watching, he picked up the bag and walked deliberately around the truck and into the open building.

The guard jerked his machine gun up, then relaxed. "I was thinking maybe you wouldn't come back," he sneered. "Then I'd have had to kill you."

Ricky glanced around as he walked up and handed

over the bag of tacos and burritos. He also dug out the change. Both workers removed their leather gloves and walked over to eat. "Diego!" one yelled. Shortly the second guard appeared by the big door and sauntered in.

Ricky turned quickly to leave.

"*Espérate!*" demanded the first guard.

Ricky stopped obediently, hoping they couldn't see him shaking.

"Did you get salsa?"

"*Sí! Sí!*" Ricky said. "*Mucha.*"

Carefully the guard dug through the bag. "I told you six burritos and eight tacos," he snapped. "Are you deaf?"

Forcing his answer, Ricky looked at the man straight. "That's what I told the man at the Restaurante San Miguel. Isn't that what he sent?"

"I think you ate one," the man snarled. "I think I should cut you open and get it!"

Ricky stepped back. "I didn't, honest I didn't."

The man swung his machine gun up. "If you aren't gone in five seconds, I'll shoot you! One . . . two . . ."

Ricky turned and raced for the door.

"Three . . . four . . ."

Ten feet left to go.

"Five!" yelled the guard.

Ricky dived out the door. A machine gun burst broke the air. Ricky landed hard in the dirt, scraping the skin on both arms. He waited to feel the bullets shred his body. Nothing. Nor did he hear any bullets hit the dirt.

Crazed laughter flooded out of the building. No longer able to see the men, Ricky picked himself up and ran around the truck to the bicycle.

He jumped on the bike, then stopped. No! Leaving was not his plan—not on the bicycle anyway. He wouldn't run. A hatred worse than anything he'd ever known held him there. If this whole thing didn't work, it wouldn't be because he'd quit. These were the people who had killed Mom—possibly the very same men. The next laugh was his, Ricky thought. Getting off the bicycle, he crawled up onto the truck's running board and waited.

The DEA complex bustled with activity. Typewriters clacked, phones rang, long-faced people hustled about. Inside a small basement room Benito Díaz shifted in his chair. The DEA director, Frank Page, sat opposite him across a large table. Several hundred photographs cluttered the varnished surface. Benito flipped wearily through another stack.

"Any of 'em look like Ricky?" mumbled Frank Page.

"Let me finish," Benito said, his temper sorely tested. He tried not to be angry, but this whole thing had been a circus from the first act. Not a single clue or sighting had panned out. Dexter Crumm had called from Mariposa, said he'd been mugged by a band of six Mexicans. Big ones, he'd said. They stole his wallet and jacket. Did some damage to his car, too. Worst of all, he'd lost his badge. Soon the agent would need rescuing, Benito mused.

The pictures in Benito's hand didn't resemble Ricky any more than the last hundred. What did these morons think Ricky was? A six-foot-tall hitchhiker? A stooped old man? A chubby kid leading a burro?

"You done?" Frank asked.

For an answer Benito slapped the pictures down like a deck of cards. He was most angry at himself. None of this would be happening if he had dealt with the León drug cartel years ago.

Frank leaned across the table and set down more pictures. "Take a look through these few more."

Benito rubbed his tired eyes. "Is someone still positioned outside the Camacho ranch?"

Frank nodded. "Not much else we can do. Today I have Buck Winslow scouring Mariposa. I assigned Dexter Crumm surveillance near the ranch—hope that's not asking for trouble." Frank Page scratched his chin. "Benito, maybe we're on the wrong path. Maybe Ricky isn't in Mexico at all."

Benito picked up the new pictures and started shuffling through them. "You're starting to sound like the others, Frank. Believe me, Ricky is there. So far I've played your game. I've been a good boy and sat here with my finger in my ear. Real soon, though, I'm going looking."

Frank kept writing on a piece of paper, showing no reaction.

One by one Benito flicked the photos completely across the table, some into Frank's lap. Nearing the end, one caught his attention. It showed a young boy walking, head down so his face wasn't visible. The black hair was too short, chopped, and unkempt. But still something about the picture looked like Ricky. The posture maybe? The kid's foot was swung forward, kicking something. Come to think of it, the skinny arms looked familiar, too. The blurry photo made it hard to tell.

Benito set the picture on the table. After finishing with the others he picked it up again.

Frank Page eyed him curiously. "Find something?"

Benito didn't answer at first. He stood and held the picture to better light. "Your guys would starve to death if they had to take photographs for a living." The boy's build and posture still held Benito's attention. He and Ricky had kicked soccer balls for many years. Ricky had a certain odd way he lowered his head and tilted a shoulder when he readied to kick. Benito's pulse raced. "Have any more pictures of this one?" he asked.

Frank Page glanced over and shook his head. "You think that one might be Ricky?"

Benito wiped a sleeve across his forehead and nodded.

Frank Page jumped to his feet. "You sure?"

"Almost positive. When was it taken?"

"Yesterday." Frank Page grabbed the photo from Benito's hand. "Let me get the guys on the mobile phone." He picked up one of several receivers on a console. "I'll try Buck Winslow first." He dialed.

Without asking, Benito picked up a second receiver and listened.

"Hello," answered a man's voice.

"Buck?" Frank Page said.

"Yeah, what's up?"

161

"We're looking here at one of the pictures you sent. We think the subject might be Sparrow Hawk. You took these pictures, right?"

"I did. Which one you looking at?"

"The subject has short-cropped hair, dirty jeans, T-shirt, and is wearing sandals, it appears. He's kicking something."

"If it's the one I'm thinking of, it's just a street kid. He kicked a can until he passed me, then quit. I remember him because not long after that I heard automatic gunfire from the direction of the Camacho ranch."

"Did he return?"

A pause. "Yeah. Yeah, he did. He was walking real fast. Wasn't kicking anything coming back. Come to think of it, he never looked up. Almost everyone stares at us like we're from outer space."

"Why didn't you report him?"

" 'Cause, well, it couldn't have been Sparrow Hawk, I don't think."

"Stand by—I'll call Dexter and ask if he's seen anything more."

"Uh, you won't need to call him. He's here in Mariposa."

"Where?"

"Right here, standing outside my car. He's had some problems."

Surprise and impatience edged Frank Page's voice. "What kind of problems? He's supposed to be out sitting surveillance."

"Here, I'll let him explain."

Again a pause.

"Hello," said a meek voice.

"That you, Dexter?"

"Uh-huh."

"Why aren't you out sitting watch?"

"I can't sit down, sir."

"You can't what?"

"I was assaulted, sir."

"Assaulted! Again? By who?"

Benito heard an awkward silence. "Uh, by a young girl, sir. A little twerp in a baggy dress. She sneaked up on my car and threw a wasp's nest in the window with a stick. I got all stung to hell, sir. Especially my rear end. I sat on some wasps when I was trying to get out."

Frank Page leaned his head back and shut his eyes as if he had a bad headache. "What did you do with her?"

"Uh, well, you see, I couldn't catch her. I tried, but the little bugger ran like a jackrabbit. Wouldn't leave me be, either. She threw rocks, damn her! I had to crawl in the car for protection. Got more stings before I could shove the wasp's nest out. Then the confounded kid kept throwing rocks until I left."

"You let a little girl chase you away from surveillance?" Frank Page nearly shouted.

"What was I supposed to do, shoot her?"

"No, you'd have probably missed! Listen, did you see a boy go past?" Frank Page described the picture again.

"Uh, yeah. One kid looked just like that. But he was riding a bicycle. I saw him turn in to the ranch."

"Did he come back out?"

"Don't know. I was, uh, forced to leave."

"But you're sure the boy headed into the compound?"

163

"Yes, sir."

"What time?"

"Oh, maybe half an hour ago."

While they talked, Benito had continued looking at the photograph in Frank Page's hand. Now he nudged Frank and pointed at the image. "It's him, Frank. I'm sure. That's Ricky!"

Frank Page squeezed his eyes closed again and shook his head. His voice tensed with frustration. "Listen, Dexter. You tell Buck that Sparrow Hawk is in the compound. We've got code orange. You hear me? Operation Sparrow Hawk is code orange!"

"Yes, sir. Should we go in after him?"

Frank Page spoke tersely. "Considering your condition, you better *stand* by."

"But, sir, I think we—"

"Hold tight till I call you back. Understand?"

"Uh-huh."

Frank Page slammed down the phone. "I was hoping I wouldn't have to call in the State Department. Looks like it's time for the big hitters."

Benito had heard all he needed. He was tired of his son being referred to as "the subject." He was tired of waiting, tired of hearing all this Sparrow Hawk garbage. And he was tired of one more thing. He was tired of being a quitter! Ricky had been right and called a duck a duck. Benito made up his mind. If his son was at the Camacho cattle ranch, he needed help, not bureaucratic foot-dragging.

"Frank, I'm going in after him with the Baby Great Lakes," Benito said. "Get me backup."

"No! Don't! I can't cover you. Our Black Hawks won't cross the border on this one."

"I said get the choppers in the air!" Benito growled. He turned and raced for the door.

"No!" shouted Frank Page. "Stop! You'll get him killed."

"We may have already done that!" Benito hollered as he broke through the front door and ran for the parking lot. His thoughts scrambled. It would take ten minutes to get out to the ranch and into the air. From there it was a crapshoot. All he'd have was his .38 revolver and the biplane. In his dictionary, that was how you spelled suicide. But if there was any chance of saving Ricky, he'd fly naked into the skies of hell.

Flies buzzing around his face annoyed Ricky. Sweat rolled down his forehead and stung his eyes. Still he waited and listened. More joking and gruff talk drifted from the big equipment shed. A small argument erupted over the food. Ricky heard cans popping open. He had no idea what the men were drinking. Paper wrinkled. Hungry grunts and fullmouthed mumbles mixed together. And then busy silence. An occasional cough or belch.

Crouched on the running board of the truck, Ricky clung to the door handle and waited. His legs began to cramp. He tried to think of what was necessary for takeoff. When his mind reached the airplane, his thoughts blanked and returned to the men inside the hangar.

"Whoooeee!" sounded a voice. "This salsa would make a burro cry!"

The other men grunted agreement and whistled low, panting aloud.

Ricky stifled a giggle. "Grab your socks. It's show time," he whispered again. If everything worked, they'd be grabbing more than their socks.

"Get me another beer," shouted the gruff guard who had shot the machine gun. "I think the fillings in my teeth are melting."

More cans popped open, and Ricky heard satisfied guzzling. He waited and hoped. Waited and hoped.

Finally, one of the men burped. "*Ooooof!* I think the salsa has melted my guts! I'll finish my beer in the outhouse."

"You don't like our company?" someone snorted. The rest laughed.

Ricky stretched up to peek through the cab windows of the truck. One of the workers stepped out the side door and strode off at a half trot. He angled away from the truck toward an outhouse on the far side of the horse corrals. Ricky had not noticed the small building earlier but was grateful now for its distant location. Impatiently he waited.

"I think it melted my guts, too!" growled a voice. "If Juan isn't done, I'll throw him out." The second worker ran out the side door and headed for the outhouse, hands gripping his stomach.

"You'll have to sit on his lap!" shouted the gruff guard after the fleeing man.

Before the second man reached the outhouse, the shortest guard raced from the shed, running with a stiff-legged gait. His machine gun bobbed up and down as he bounded along. His desperation made him rigid.

Ricky felt tension growing inside his stomach as he waited. What if the big guard with the farmer coveralls hadn't eaten any of the food? Maybe he was so fat the arrow weed had no effect. "C'mon," Ricky begged silently. Almost at once his request was answered.

"Hijo!" bellowed the last guard. "There's fire in my belly!" Swearing loudly, the burly ox weaved out of the building. He ran knock-kneed, swinging his machine gun with one hand, the other hand clamped tightly under his britches.

Down by the outhouse a fight broke out. The second man yanked open the door and hauled the first worker off the seat and shoved him stumbling into some prickly pear cactus. The worker bawled with pain even as he struggled to his feet to continue his chore. The third man hopped up and down, howling at the sky and pleading for his turn.

The largest guard ambled into the fray like a bulldozer. "Open the door and get off!" he screamed. "My turn!" He fired his machine gun into the air to make his point. "Hurry!" With a grunt, he pulled the other guard off the seat. The two started wrestling in the dirt, throwing punches. The first guard's pants remained down, hobbling his ankles. While the two brawled, one of the workers crept inside and jumped on the valued hole.

"You lizard!" screamed the biggest guard, breaking off the fight. He jerked and pulled on the locked door.

Ricky jolted into action. He jumped to the ground and raced for the shop door, his cramped legs tingling. The last thing he saw over his shoulder was two men pushing over the outhouse, occupant and all. Ricky ran directly to the plane and kicked the blocks from under the tires. He tried the door. It was locked. He glanced about, frantic. In a far corner sat a small desk. Ricky ran and jerked open the drawers. Nothing. Think, he told himself. Slow down and think!

A green metal cabinet hung over the desk. Ricky pulled open a door. On a board lined with nails hung nearly a dozen sets of keys. He rifled through them. Each had a tag on the key ring: DC-3, Mojave, Beech, Bell 1, Bell 2, Bell 3, 172. Ricky grabbed the 172 keys.

Fingers awkward with haste, he unlocked and opened the Skyhawk door. The rear seat had been removed, and the right passenger's seat was turned to face a big black console and radar screen in the back. Behind the pilot's seat was wedged a large cardboard box. The lettering read Baby Diapers.

Loud swearing and shouts from the distressed men still echoed in the distance. Ricky knew he needed to hurry. Yet if he didn't do everything right, he could crash. Did he dare take time to check the gas, oil, tires, brakes, and other things outside? No, he decided. Worse yet, once the engine started, he wouldn't be able to wait and check oil pressure or magnetos, or allow for warm-up. This was what Dad called a forced crapshoot.

Scrambling in, Ricky closed the door. His fingers were sweating as he fumbled to insert the key. He held his breath. It fitted. Most of the instruments and controls looked similar to the Cessna 150 he trained in. He found the fuel switch and turned it to ON. Carefully he flipped the master switch and heard the familiar quiet whine.

He twisted the control yoke and kicked on the rudder pedals—they seemed to be free. Again he let his eyes sweep across the instruments. Spotting the fuel mixture control, he pushed it to RICH.

He snugged the seat belt tight. Fuel gauges showed mostly full. What else? Had he forgotten anything? Maybe it would help to prime the engine with fuel. But how much? Too little, and it would not start. Too much would flood it. Hand shaking, he pushed the prime plunger one full stroke.

Wiping his palms on his dirty pants, Ricky looked straight ahead. As soon as he cleared the big shed, he would be visible from the outhouse. There would be no time to taxi down and use the full runway. Takeoff toward the compound would give him the most distance and be into the wind. Even that might not be enough.

Well, this was it. Mouth dry as dirt, hands trembling, Ricky turned the ignition to START.

23

The propeller flopped over with a *thup, thup, thup, thup,* but the engine didn't catch. Ricky kept the starter grinding and quickly pumped in more fuel with the primer. The engine coughed. Twice more the prop flopped over, then belched to life. As the throttle was pushed in full, a deafening roar erupted.

Chairs, jackets, rakes, loose marijuana, and anything else in the shed not bolted down whipped and smashed into the walls. Shuddering, the Skyhawk lurched forward. Ricky searched the instrument panel. Oil pressure looked good. Flaps were up. Nobody had appeared around the shed yet. He could not see back into the hangar.

The low seat made it hard to see out. Ahead the taxiway ended. The Skyhawk rolled faster and faster. Ricky knew he'd have to swerve onto the runway without slowing. A sharp turn could scrape a wing and throw him out of control. Approaching the turn, Ricky stomped on the rudder pedal and twisted the yoke so the airplane's control surfaces would help steer. Any speed carried through the corner would shorten the takeoff.

The plane veered, and Ricky fought for control. A tire lifted off the ground, and the wing dipped dangerously toward the runway. He couldn't turn any sharper. Refusing to back off the throttle, he let the plane swerve wide. The hovering tire dropped back to the runway as the Skyhawk straightened, its nose pointed down the grass strip. Slowly, too slowly, the speed built.

"C'mon!" Ricky pleaded. "C'mon!"

The plane bounced and jolted along. Looking back, Ricky caught movement from the corner of his eye. The shortest guard had hobbled around the corner of the equipment shed. He held his pants up with one hand. The other hand brandished his machine gun. Ricky could not hear shots, but he could see bursts of fire leaping out of the barrel. Gravel spit up alongside the Skyhawk.

The end of the runway seemed to race toward him. He had to go faster—trying to take off too soon would make him crash. Ricky forced himself to leave the yoke forward and let the Skyhawk have its run. The big guard joined the first beside the shed. Stumbling, and with his coveralls drooped around his knees, he raised his machine gun. Again Ricky saw bursts of gunfire.

Plumes of dust kicked up ahead. Gravel, or maybe a bullet, stung the plane. A long crack appeared across the windshield. Now the end of the runway was only seconds away. "C'mon, please go faster!" Ricky prayed. A sharp *twang* rocked the plane. Bullet holes had stitched parallel patterns up the cockpit wall. Ricky's thoughts raced, and he looked wildly out the windshield. A bullet to the engine, gas tank, or tire would finish him. The Skyhawk bounced as it hit rough gravel at the end of the runway.

"Now!" Ricky screamed. He drew back on the yoke. For a heartbeat the Skyhawk clung to the gravel, then lifted free. The plane skimmed the desert floor, airspeed too slow for climb-out. Ricky's voice was hoarse with fear. "Go! Go! Go!" He banked gradually away from the equipment shed to give the guards less of a target. He expected, at any second, a burst of gunfire to riddle his body. He could imagine the Skyhawk cartwheeling across the desert in a bright ball of flames.

Ricky held his breath and watched the airspeed indicator. Seventy-five miles per hour, eighty miles per hour, eighty-five. Now ninety. Streaking low to the ground, the plane was building precious airspeed. It also made a more difficult target. At a hundred miles per hour, Ricky eased the nose up into a shallow climb.

On the ground two Jeeps were visible, racing toward the big shed. Gunfire flashed like firecrackers. This far away the bullets should fall short. The Jeeps pulled to a stop. Ricky could seen men running for the choppers. He kept climbing.

Purposely he banked toward the western edge of Mariposa. As the checkerboard city blocks passed underneath, he rocked his wings sharply. Once, twice, three times, four times. Then he leveled. He hoped a very special pair of eyes was watching.

The thought of Soledad brought a lump to his throat. Cripes, he felt guilty leaving her. They had sure done a bunch of crazy stuff. He couldn't wait to tell Dad about her. Never again would he call a begging kid a *ratero*.

Still climbing, Ricky banked north toward the border. At a thousand feet he leveled and headed for their landing strip back home. Dad and the DEA could do anything they wanted with the plane now. Ricky looked back at the shiny black radar and grinned. He'd done it! He'd really done it! What would Dad say?

From habit he reached for the dash and turned on the radio, setting the frequency to 122.4, the one he and Dad always used. The familiar number was comforting, although today Dad would not be around.

The engine droned. Ricky checked the instruments carefully. So far, so good! He looked up beyond the clouds, beyond the sky, and beyond the blue. "Can you believe it, Mamá?" he said.

She failed to appear.

"I did it, Mamá! I really did it!" he said louder.

No image appeared, nor did he hear her voice. Still he smiled. It was okay now, he didn't mind. He would never forget her, but she didn't need to answer him all the time. He could quit bugging her.

Ricky guessed he had forty or fifty miles left before entering U.S. airspace. Were the men who ran toward the helicopters the pilots? Could they possibly catch him? Every few miles he banked so he could look behind and search the southern sky.

The Skyhawk seemed to fly so slowly. Yet the airspeed read over a hundred and twenty miles per hour. With growing anxiety, Ricky watched the clock on the instrument panel. Fifteen long minutes passed. The border could be only another ten miles now at most. One last time Ricky banked. At first he saw nothing. Then, squinting higher into the sun, he glimpsed a dark pod! No, two! Three! The Bell helicopters from Rancho Camacho flew stacked in formation, closing fast.

Ricky panicked. He started to climb, but his airspeed dwindled. The Bell Rangers could go faster, outclimb, and outmaneuver the Skyhawk. If only Dad were here, he'd know what to do. But Ricky knew he was alone. Today Dad would be no help.

In minutes the first of the choppers swung alongside. Ricky saw that the side door was removed. A man in a harness hung halfway out, a machine gun slung from his shoulder. He turned and aimed.

Ricky shoved the control yoke hard. The Skyhawk dived sharply. The helicopter disappeared, the deafening *whup, whup, whup* of its blades fading upward. In a forced dive, the loose diaper box behind Ricky's seat rose off the floor and floated magically about the cabin like the marshmallows had years ago in training. Then the box slid forward next to the passenger's door as Ricky leveled. This time the chopper pilot had been outmaneuvered and would have to set up before the door guard could get another shot.

Out of nowhere the second chopper moved in. This one also had a gunner perched in the open. Ricky banked the Skyhawk sharply to the right. The chopper banked with him.

Now the third Bell moved in close below, blocking another dive. The big blades whipped within yards of the Skyhawk, causing it to bounce and shake. Ricky's eyes fell on the diaper box that had slid up from behind his seat. Maybe it held something besides diapers. He reached over and pulled open the top. Inside were nearly a dozen white bricks. Ricky wondered if it was packaged cocaine. He remained above the lower chopper. Flipping the window vent open, he pitched one of the heavy bricks into the airstream. The white material was not flour, and the target was not a saguaro cactus. But the idea was the same. And this time there was more at stake than a milk shake.

Ricky knew the chopper's occupants could not see what was happening. Deliberately he descended, closer. With luck, some of the bricks would hit one of the big rotor blades. He tossed another and another. The fourth brick exploded in a cloud of white. The chopper rocked. It held its place, but the hollow *whup, whup, whup* of the blades grew uneven. Ricky kept shoving bricks out the window. He laughed in triumph as another brick smacked a blade with a dull *whap*.

The helicopter was still beneath him as Ricky's fingers closed on the last waxy brick. Ricky dived nearly into the chopper blade. "Take this!" he yelled.

Whap! Again a cloud of white exploded. A deafening knock echoed up as the chopper veered off. The last Ricky saw, the pilot was losing altitude, fighting for control.

Now there were no more bricks. Raw panic ripped at Ricky's gut. With one helicopter covering his side and the other waiting above, he was a sitting duck. He had altitude enough for maybe two more dives. Then what?

Again the second chopper banked in close, and the gunner swung his weapon around to fire.

The radio crackled with static. Ricky dived again as fire spit from the machine gun. The chopper anticipated the move and dived with him, not letting him get away. Ricky pulled back and climbed, but the chopper shadowed him. The chopper flew so close that a wicked grin could be seen parting the gunner's lips.

"Loop it, Ricky! Loop it!" The garbled words came out of nowhere. They startled Ricky. Was it the radio or his mind?

"Loop it!" Benito's voice crackled from the radio.

The machine gun flashed. Something splintered behind the seat.

"I'm coming, *mi 'jito*!" Benito yelled over the radio. "I got you in sight. But I need a few seconds. If you hear me, crank a loop. Those choppers can't loop. But you're low, so don't waffle it!"

Ricky crammed the yoke forward, standing the Skyhawk on its nose in a sharp dive for airspeed. Could he loop the Skyhawk? Was there enough altitude? "Papá!" he screamed, not picking up the handset. He searched the sky. Where was Dad? Ricky could not see the last two choppers, but he knew both were near. The airspeed needle shot up into the red zone. The ground raced up.

Ricky pulled back hard, rocketing out of the dive, up into a body-crushing climb. His grip did not waver. He pulled harder and brought the plane over onto its back. This is how Soledad would loop if she knew how. He might end up without wings, but he would not waffle it.

177

Maps, pencils, dust, and cigarette ashes tumbled to the ceiling. The engine faltered. And quit! Ricky pulled harder. The Skyhawk didn't have an inverted fuel system. With the air windmilling the propeller, the engine should start when it came back upright. Airspeed picked up, whining and buffeting the plane. Worst of all, Ricky saw the ground—much too close—coming straight at him. He strained against the yoke. Black spots danced across his eyes. He felt his cheeks sag. His chin pressed against his chest.

"Pull back! You're going in!" screamed Benito.

Ricky had never heard his dad yell over the radio. The sound carried a deadly urgency. He braced himself and willed every muscle to focus on one thing: the yoke. And through a clouded blackness, Ricky strained. Pull, he told himself. Fight the darkness! Fight it! A flicker of light splashed across his consciousness. He blinked desperately, unable to see the ground. But the ground was there. And it wanted to kill him.

With a deafening whine, the engine roared back to life.

"Whoeeee! You did it, Ricky! You did it!" Benito yelled.

Ricky eased up on the yoke. His vision cleared as he leveled the plane right side up. The ground blurred past, barely a hundred feet below. Ricky grabbed up the handset. "The lizards ducked on that one!" he screamed, his voice giddy with fear.

"Got their tails trimmed," Benito said, chuckling. "Listen, *mi 'jito*, they're faster than us. You climb toward the border. I'll see how these clowns like a dogfight!"

Full throttle, Ricky started climbing. If only he had the power of the Baby. Again he picked up the handset. He keyed the microphone so he could be heard. "Papá, where are you? Where are you, Papá?"

A helicopter banked around, lining up again on the Skyhawk.

"Right here!" shouted Benito. A roaring red flash sliced the sky from above. The helicopter veered sharply to avoid being smashed by the growling Baby Great Lakes.

Ricky heard his dad's voice, cold and deliberate. "We have a score to settle, boys."

24

Ricky climbed the Skyhawk, coaxing it upward with a tight grip on the yoke. When he risked a glance back, the Camacho choppers had swung into formation, guarding each other. The bright red Baby Great Lakes winged over and spiraled into them. They scattered. One chopper banked around, pursuing Ricky. Benito snapped the Baby upward and twisted in on a collision course. For a moment the chopper held its heading. The red biplane closed, the big radial engine snarling like a mad dog. At the last second the helicopter veered nearly out of control to avoid the attack. Never before had Ricky seen his dad fly this wildly.

For the moment the helicopters had no advantage. Their extra speed only helped them run from the attacking biplane. The Baby Great Lakes badgered them, looping, rolling, diving, and twisting. The choppers flew in confused patterns.

With the dogfight too distant to keep watching, Ricky returned his attention to the cockpit. The altimeter showed nearly two thousand feet. Ahead and to the east stretched the border town of Domingo.

"Ricky Díaz," crackled a strange voice over the radio, "we have you in sight. This is DEA Black Hawk leader six-niner-seven. Continue north, heading three-five-two. Do you read?"

Ricky combed the horizon. There they were—five Black Hawk helicopters hovering near the border! They looked menacing in a tight line, three hundred feet off the ground. Ricky picked up the handset. "Roger, DEA."

"Ricky!" Benito broke in. "These jokers just got smart. They've separated and are coming at you from different directions. I can't hold 'em both. Start diving. Trade in your altitude for speed. You hear me? Dive!"

Before Ricky could answer, Black Hawk leader crackled back, "Ricky, this is Black Hawk six-niner-seven. Dive toward us. You're safe once you cross the border, guaranteed!"

Ricky felt sweat running down his temples. His arms had started cramping. He shoved the control yoke forward, starting a shallow dive. With full power the engine wailed. Wind screeched past the wings. It wasn't good for an airplane to dive full power. Ricky knew this. But getting shot full of holes wasn't exactly good for a plane either. Desperately he aimed the streaking Skyhawk toward the hovering DEA choppers.

"Keep her coming, keep her coming," coaxed the stranger in the Black Hawk. "Never thought I'd see Sparrow Hawk Red!"

What was this Sparrow Hawk Red stuff? Ricky wondered. He kept the dive angled toward the DEA choppers. The altimeter needle swung under a thousand feet. Air whistled through the bullet holes behind the seat. Half a mile to go!

"Keep diving, Ricky," the formation leader shouted. "One of those snakes is on your tail. Come in underneath us. If the bogey continues, he's bacon!"

Ricky dared not look around. He concentrated on the narrow gap of sky below the choppers as it raced up at him with dizzying speed. The Skyhawk was coming in hot!

"Bring her home, Sparrow Hawk. Bring her home," coached the voice, brittle with tension.

Ricky tasted blood from biting his lip. The Black Hawks and the ground blurred past as he rocketed under the formation.

Black Hawk leader suddenly laughed aloud. "You're home, Sparrow Hawk! Our bogey skipped the party. Didn't want his candles lit."

Ricky pulled from his dive in a long screaming arc. The end choppers peeled from formation and pulled alongside. Both pilots waved, their faces hidden by helmets and dark visors.

"Way to go, Sparrow Hawk," one called over the radio. "That's some flying!"

"Why do you call me Sparrow Hawk?" Ricky asked.

"Guess you wouldn't know that," the pilot's voice crackled. "It's been your code name through this whole operation. I'm sure looking forward to meeting you."

Ricky smiled, looking down at his ragged clothes and car-tire sandals. The guy would swallow his tonsils and think he was a . . . Ricky stopped himself from thinking *ratero*—nobody was a street rat. The guy would think he was a homeless beggar.

"Would you follow us?" the pilot asked.

"Not without my dad," Ricky answered.

"Fair enough. We'll make an easy three-hundred-sixty-degree circle left. Your dad should be here any minute. Sparrow Hawk, how is your fuel?"

Ricky flashed the pilot a thumbs-up okay. He banked easily about, the two Black Hawks shadowing his wings.

"Sparrow Hawk, you got any kind of radar aboard?"

Ricky smiled. "Yup, just happened to have one in the back. A *big* one." He thought of the agent's badge in his pocket. "Black Hawk six-niner-zero."

"Go ahead, Sparrow Hawk."

"I have one of your agents' badges, too. The name is Dexter Crumm."

The stranger's voice he'd heard earlier came on. "Sparrow Hawk, this is DEA director Frank Page. Please repeat what you said on Dexter Crumm."

"I got his badge!"

"You can't. Dexter lost that to six men who mugged him on some back street."

"Baloney!" Ricky exclaimed. "I snitched it from him 'cause he was looking for me."

The man chuckled. "I'll be anxious to hear the whole story when we land. A disciplinary review board might enjoy hearing it, too."

183

"Mind if I join you?" Benito broke in over the radio. The Baby Great Lakes streaked past like greased red lightning.

Ricky grinned, watching the shiny biplane screw barrel rolls upward through the sky. Sun glinted off the twin wings. Benito looped the red Baby over into a long, sweeping victory roll around the formation. The maneuver settled him into perfect position beside the right chopper. He waggled his wings and gave a thumbs-up to the formation. "Good afternoon, gents," he said casually.

Ricky dipped his own wings and flashed his thumb back. Jeez, this was great! He caught his dad's broad smile. They flew without speaking.

Finally Benito spoke. "That was sure some flying you did, *mi 'jito!*"

"You taught me," Ricky answered proudly.

"Not to fly like that, I didn't."

"You taught me not to be a quitter."

There was an awkward pause. Benito's voice broke the stillness. "I should have listened to my own advice."

Again they flew in silence. Ricky spoke next. "Papá, I'm going to need your help."

"What's wrong?"

"I made a good friend in Mariposa. Somehow I have to help her—will you go back with me later?"

"I'd love to, *mi 'jito.* By the way, how would you like to help me out?"

"Doing what?"

"Oh, I just thought if I started flying air shows again, I'd need someone along I could trust."

184

"Are you kidding?"

"Not on your life. Well, are you up for it?"

"You bet," Ricky said, grinning. He watched the last three Black Hawks swing in and join the formation. The five helicopters, the Baby Great Lakes, and the Skyhawk were flying in a rough V, Ricky at the point.

"Sparrow Hawk," Black Hawk leader broke in. "We'd be honored to escort you to Cooper Air Base for debriefing."

Ricky looked at the helicopter separating him from Benito. "Only if Papá can be my wingman," he answered, his voice firm.

"No problem," the pilot answered. He rolled out of position.

Benito swung the Baby in tight beside the Skyhawk. He nodded to Ricky, his head bowed. "I'd be honored to be your wingman, Son!"

BEN MIKAELSEN lives with his wife, Melanie, and a six-hundred-pound bear named Buffy in Bozeman, Montana. His first book for young readers, *Rescue Josh McGuire,* won both the Western Writers of America Spur Award and the International Reading Association's Best First Work Award. In researching *Sparrow Hawk Red,* Mr. Mikaelsen spent time among the homeless children of Mexico and drew upon his own childhood experiences growing up in Bolivia, South America. He has also spent many hours at the controls of a Cessna 150 and a Cessna 172 while earning his pilot's license.